SOLOMON'S FOLLY

Solomon Grimaud is a Jewish millionaire living in
late nineteenth-century Alexandria. His white villa,
with its Empire furniture and tiered gardens, over-
looks the Mediterranean, and from it he can observe
and admire the passage of his fleet of cotton ships.
Yet he has paid a high price for success. In adopting
the ideals of self-sufficiency and progress he has
sacrificed the tender side of his personality. Only
when faced with personal and financial disaster does
he find the courage to reconstitute his personality
into a wiser, sadder one. But Grimaud's discarded
beliefs have not relaxed their hold, for his son has
adopted them as the model for his own life and is
prepared to sacrifice all scruples—perhaps even his
father's life—to ambitions which he has been taught
are morally inviolable.

D1626298

SOLOMON'S FOLLY

by

LESLIE CROXFORD

1974

CHATTO & WINDUS

LONDON

Published by
Chatto & Windus Ltd
42 William IV Street
London WC2N 4DF

*

Clarke, Irwin & Co Ltd
Toronto

ISBN 0 7011 2035 5

© Leslie Croxford 1974

Printed in Great Britain by
Ebenezer Baylis & Son Limited
The Trinity Press, Worcester, and London

To Leo

CONTENTS

Book One

Book Two

Book One

Book One

PART I

The Late 1870s

A Client Dies

Chapter 1

At first there were only isolated outbreaks of violence. They happened in the late afternoon when Europeans strayed into the poorer parts of Alexandria. A group of Arabs would be lounging outside their mud huts, watching the limestone track which had burnt their feet all day, as it blackened in the dusk. Or else nursing bamboo fly swats, and idly stroking horse-tails which hung from the handles, they might argue and talk while the outline faded from the surrounding quarries at Mex.

Suddenly an Arab would whip at a mosquito flying into a remnant of sunlight. Carefully picking it from the white hair, his eyes became blank as the insect floated to the ground. After a period of silence, in which nothing could be heard except the constant droning of blue-bottles and the distant wash of the sea, he noticed the smart crunch of footsteps.

This evening several Arabs turned, without moving their shoulders, to observe a stranger approaching. His white jacket flapped over a dark waistcoat; the lapels disarranged his bow-tie. They saw him stand still, directly before them; and the middle-aged gentleman, wiping his flushed cheeks with a red polka dot handkerchief, inserted a finger between his wing collar and neck.

'Hey mister! You lost?' The European responded by glancing at the Egyptian through the misted pince-nez that were settled precariously on his nose. Then pulling down his straw hat and continuing to walk he heard the question repeated more loudly. He did not care to turn back.

In earlier months the stranger would have been allowed to pass on, growing more and more lost in the maze of identical houses and streets. Europeans, still unaware of the hostility they excited, entered the Arab quarter in sufficient numbers to discourage open assaults. But as the 1870s wore on, a stranger would almost certainly have been attacked from behind. The gentleman's pince-nez were suddenly pulled from his face. He roamed about in the unfocused night.

By now he was shouting out. He threatened to fetch the police. He called all Arabs vermin and swine. Yet his voice rattled round empty roads until it merged with the dry cough of a beggar and the purring of cats making their delicate ways through the gutter.

'Death to the Nasrani!' An Egyptian pursued him down an alley. He spat and pushed him against a wall. Battering his head against the dried mud he picked up an old bottle. The others gazed distantly on.

Bodies were often found dumped on the beach. Some lay at the bottom of pits where rats fed on the scraps of fish and meat thrown down from the markets.

Europeans requested protection. Eminent businessmen, claiming to represent whole national communities, presented themselves—unannounced—in consular offices. Some travelled to Cairo to demand interviews with their harassed ambassadors on the basis of slight social connections.

In time foreign papers agitated for punitive measures. The cause of Egyptian Nationalism was bogus; its leader, Arabi Pacha, was an obvious demagogue. Certain members of Queen Victoria's government were reminded of the recent Bulgarian atrocities. Even Mr. Gladstone, who had long prevaricated, agreed in principle with the policy outlined by the French Premier, Gambetta: the stability of Egypt was a matter of both British and French concern.

A CLIENT DIES

Chapter 2

Pierre LeGrand, general practitioner, was awakened by
the sound of knocking on the front door of his flat. At first
the noise seemed to be part of a muffled dream but by the
time he had got out of bed the maid was holding a lamp
and calling out from the veranda:

'It's the police!'

'Now don't get so excited. Go back to bed.' Yet
minutes later, having hurriedly dressed and joined the two
Arab policemen in their cab, he could still see the girl's
swarthy face lit up at the third floor window.

LeGrand tried to insert his collar stud as the horse
pulled away. After struggling with it for a few moments,
the metal broke in his fingers. He cursed and stroking his
double chin sighed as he rolled up the black tie in his
pocket. He relapsed into silence as he often did after
summoning up the necessary burst of energy on these
nocturnal calls. He listened to the rhythmical clink of the
harness, thankful for the breeze which their movement
brought to the stifling air.

It was some way from his flat to the alley where a dead
man had been discovered. They rode swiftly through the
city, passing the stationary trams on the Boulevard
Ramleh, leaving the equestrian figure of Mohammed Ali
far behind. They moved down the long wide promenade
which ran parallel to the sea. It was quite empty on this
moonless night. Only the slight lights of stars were visible
through the open hood of the cab. The area illumined by
their unsteady lamp added shape to the sounds of water
and the clatter of wheels on the flagstones.

The policemen began talking in Arabic. One of them
offered the Doctor a cigarette. LeGrand refused, turning
to rest a cheek on his hand and touching the red birth-
mark which covered one side of his face. He wiped away
the sweat which had broken onto its surface and gazed
into the surrounding void.

While he sat rocking in the carriage he saw the night

11

yield up the dark shapes of palm leaves; they vaulted the esplanade at regular intervals. He wished the policemen would stop discharging the raucous sounds of which he imagined that he was the subject. As if indifferent he yawned without covering his mouth.

Then suddenly exhausted, he asked himself why he had consented to ride through the city in the early hours of the morning to see a corpse that he could do nothing to revive.

LeGrand had often been called in the middle of the night. He was used to the anxious faces of relatives who ushered him up shadowy staircases and through gloomy halls. He would enter bedrooms where the smell of a single candle mixed with the odour of medicines and old bedclothes. Yet the older he grew the harder he tried to relay advice through the servants who had been sent as messengers, and the more mechanically he took patients' pulses.

Years ago he had longed for excitement once his evening surgery was over. There had been dinner, the theatre, friends. But he had never married, and nowadays he usually stayed in the empty flat. The maid propped herself up against the kitchen door and stood staring at her vacant master.

The cab was now moving more and more slowly. They had just passed from the Boulevard to the Arab quarter. The horse picked its way from flagstones to cobbles. Then, scarcely progressing at all among huts built so near together that they formed tunnels rather than roads, the animal's hooves thudded on dry earth. LeGrand sat with his head back, a handkerchief pressed to his nose, trying to obliterate the sickeningly sweet smell of garbage and the odours of urine and mud.

Later the movement ceased altogether in a slight widening of the way. The policemen jumped out smartly and greeted two colleagues who were waiting by a primitive fountain. LeGrand did not follow them down immediately. He was watching the brass spout bursting with water, so tired that the present felt like a dream.

'Doctor!' Instinctively following the voice, he dismounted. 'Doctor!' He pursued it along an alley. LeGrand lagged further and further behind the others; he wiped his forehead with a shining sleeve. He was coughing by the time they had reached an open expanse. It took him several seconds to realize that they were standing on the harbour by Mex.

'It's over there,' the senior policeman said, pointing. They crossed to the customs shed. A guard was standing by a long white bundle just outside the door. 'It was only dumped here. He was killed,' LeGrand heard for the second time, 'in an alley in the Arab quarter.'

The Doctor knelt down to look at the body. The air was heavy and hot. He heard the metal stud at the end of his shoe echo through the dockyard. Then, removing the sheet, he was overpowered by a smell of manure rising from the area which was daily used as a cab-rank. LeGrand did not notice the head immediately. But when he leant over it, his fingers touched something sharp. It was a piece of glass embedded in the temple: there was a thick stain around the wound: and blood, soaking through the silver hair, had darkened into a crust.

'He was hit with this.' LeGrand looked up. The police-man pointed to the jagged remnants of a wine bottle. A pair of spectacles, with a bent frame and cracked lenses, lay beside it on the ground. Turning back to the corpse the Doctor noticed shreds of a polka dot handkerchief clasped in its fist. For a moment he thought he recognized the face, but the dense fluid had separated out into blackish patches, disfiguring an entire cheek.

LeGrand fingered the side of his face as they walked into the customs shed. Standing near a lamp in the office, sur-rounded by packing cases and ledgers, he began shivering and had to lean against a table to steady himself.

The senior policeman, watched with childlike fascina-tion by the others, was spreading out forms. He dipped a pen into the inkwell and politely offered it to the Doctor. LeGrand again felt a wave of faintness; he was almost overcome by the smell of pigment and tobacco on the officer's breath.

'Is there a chair?' he asked in a weak voice.

He must have been writing for longer than he realized. By the time they had left the shed it was almost light. The water was grey enough for LeGrand to see the reddish patches of oil which formed on its surface. Walking along the dock side he noticed the yellow teeth of a rat floating face up among the drift-wood.

Soon, for no apparent reason, the Doctor found himself thinking of darkness rather than dawn. He had an image of two men sitting in a shadowy alcove. One was Solomon Grimaud, a wealthy businessman whose family he had often treated. The Doctor had been lingering in a café near the Rue Rosette that very evening when he had seen him enter with a client. M. Grimaud's companion had been flushed, corpulent, and middle-aged. The light had glinted on his pince-nez . . . The Doctor shuddered. He had just recognized the dead man.

LeGrand felt unreal as he made his way from the half-light back through the darkened streets. Just before following the police into the cab he washed his head at the fountain, dousing his face again and again.

His limbs seemed to be floating when they re-entered the boulevard. His head buzzed but it could have been the jangle of the harness, or the noise of the gathering crowd. Only the wail of the muezzin pierced the persistent drone. Like the sound of a tortured creature it spread from high on a gleaming tower. The cry carried over the city, beyond the houses and streets. And as LeGrand turned from the esplanade it was lost in the brilliant blue of the sea.

Chapter 3

LeGrand often visited the café near the Rue Rosette after his evening surgery. Having chatted with his patients, allowing himself the slight immodesty of pointing out that unlike most doctors he wrote his prescriptions in a legible copper-plate hand, he felt in need of further company. He would go out to play draughts over an aperitif with Daniel Benchimol, a Sephardic schoolmaster whom he had treated for a liver complaint.

LeGrand found time to day-dream between moves, for young Benchimol would speak of an intellectual ferment in Paris; he intended to take his poems and stories to a French publisher as soon as circumstances permitted.

'Really, one shouldn't let adversity worry one. The artist must have the strength of will to grasp his ideal, in spite'—he wagged a finger at LeGrand—'of his material conditions. For example, when I refused to work in my father's business in Lyons . . .'

He turned back to the board as the Doctor took three of his pieces and added them to a neat stack.

Occasionally, if there was no school in the afternoon, they might have tea at the Hotel Cecil. LeGrand insisted on spending some time choosing their place, for although they wished to sit in the shade he also wanted to see the people who were visiting Alexandria. Watching ladies talking in large hats, perspiring beneath their veils, Benchimol and the Doctor tried to guess where each was from. The young lady sitting by the piano was Viennese, and the one shaded by the potted palm surely came from St. Petersburg. While the old woman wearing violet and silver undoubtedly lived in London, together with the pinched, elderly companion who pushed her black invalid chair.

LeGrand lingered long after the gold rimmed cups had been removed. He yawned as his companion spoke of his plans for travelling once his writing had been acclaimed. He dozed for a while, still thinking himself in Byzantium on waking: and waiters in red fezes made their deft ways through cool colonnades.

LeGrand continued listening to the small orchestra, long after Benchimol had left. He watched the fountain, while they played out-of-tune waltzes which he had first heard as a student in Paris. As he remembered his old ambition to become a great scientist, the water gradually darkened. So with legs numbed, he turned from the tumbling moonlight and walked through the metal gates.

Thank God that at least the Doctor had close friends like Daniel Benchimol! LeGrand invariably consoled himself with the thought, in a solitary hour after tea, when overcome by moods of futility and despair. Though the two of them rarely conversed, and had few obvious interests in common, he felt sure that there was a bond of tacit understanding born of the interaction of maturity and youth.

If he also felt that they had been thrown together less out of mutual respect and more as a relief for one another's sense of isolation, he would dismiss the idea as a regrettable symptom of his middle-aged wariness of true friendship. While glancing into the darkness, Daniel's face, with its strong jaw and wide forehead, seemed to grow quite clear in LeGrand's mind: the Doctor pensively stroked his blemished cheek and, half realizing it, smiled.

In time, as he continued thinking, LeGrand might find that Daniel's features were being metamorphosed. They were assuming the contours of another patient's face. The gentleman, Solomon Grimaud, and Benchimol hardly looked similar; yet their bearings as a whole seemed to share some common quality. Was it arrogance or ambition the Doctor wondered. Certainly it was a strength of personality which he knew that he lacked.

LeGrand often found himself associating people with each other. Resemblances occurred to him for reasons which he could hardly explain. For example, fathers and sons—like M. Grimaud, say, and his young Albert— were surely alike in more than a physical sense. There was a kind of boldness, a certain intensity, typical of both the parent and child.

It might be interesting to see, LeGrand reflected, how far Albert would merely inherit his father's character, together with his fortune. Would the boy ever proclaim a substantial independence of M. Grimaud? Then yawning, the Doctor checked himself for asking the hypothetical question which he had senselessly posed about every baby he had ever delivered. It was best not to toy with insoluble problems. No clear answers existed. Again he peered into the dark.

The Doctor often had an opportunity of seeing Albert with his father. He was usually summoned to the Grimauds' villa at night. LeGrand would walk to the Boulevard Ramleh and join the crowd which always milled about the trams. There he competed with figures dressed in black, women carrying cages of live chickens, and Coptic priests from a nearby church.

As they approached Chatby he looked into the darkness which appeared to hover over the dry flats. He considered how many of his patients had been consigned to its graves. Then passing out of the noisy city, as the tram emptied with each successive stop, he caught himself thinking of the ruined cemeteries, laid out in the night, containing the buried bones of ancient heroes.

Soon the tram arrived at Ibrahimieh, and from then on, to the right, there was rich, black delta mud. There were wide fig trees and tall palms, and beyond them great spaces of stars. On and on the horses clinked in their harnesses till he could smell the eucalyptus and pine. Against his face he felt the cool sea breezes rising up from the private gardens at Ramleh.

It was only a short walk from the tram stop to M. Grimaud's house. It stood, together with the other European villas, well back from the road. Shadowy cypresses quivered on either side of the carriage sweep and gave way to orange trees growing by the marble steps. As LeGrand climbed the stairs bougainvillaea, their tendrils trained around six white pillars, nodded gently and continued their fragile movement when he entered the house.

On occasion LeGrand was asked to wait for a moment in a niche attached to the spacious hall. M. Grimaud, who would say that he had almost finished speaking to a business client, frequently wished to discuss his wife's mysterious, lingering illness in the study before, as well as after, the Doctor visited Mme Grimaud. So LeGrand would cast an eye over water-colours of Napoleon's

Egyptian victories. They depicted the battle of the Pyramids, the engagement at Aboukir. He might sit in a reddish-brown arm-chair of the same period, resting his fingers on the gold eagle's head. For a while he looked at the other furniture, decorated with gilt sphinxes and Imperial designs; but then, feeling he had been kept waiting for too long, he asked himself if he should not at least have been shown to the drawing-room. Yet what else could one expect from a Jewish cotton merchant? Wasn't he too unrefined to appreciate . . .

He would regain his calm in the instant that Grimaud appeared with his client.

'Now I want you to meet the best doctor in the whole of Egypt.' LeGrand put a hand to his neck and smiled.

LeGrand always enjoyed the attention which Grimaud showed him after he had examined his wife. A servant would enter the drawing-room carrying a silver tray filled with cigarettes—Turkish, Black Russians—and every kind of cigar. The Doctor found it relaxing to sip the warmed brandy, lounging among curtains and covers made of Damascus silk. It was fine to talk, if only of illness, to a man whose position was so secure in the world. Later they would talk in the garden; it was built in tiers overlooking the sea. LeGrand's step gradually became more and more certain; and watching their cigar smoke drifting below them, they paused to look in the evening at the slight curve formed by Stanley Bay.

So then LeGrand might think of Grimaud as a friend. He placed his arm for a moment around his broad shoulders: he would be laughing as that harmonious face, with its well-trimmed black beard, made sardonic comments about the Arab character. Then having re-entered the noiseless house to collect his bag, the Doctor stopped in the hallway, smelling the scented furniture polish, noticing the honeycomb candles reflected in the smooth floor tiles.

Sauntering back to the tram stop, thinking that he might grow a beard to hide his birth-mark, LeGrand felt it had been an enjoyable evening. He did not mind standing a full twenty minutes before the horse-drawn vehicle lumbered up beside him. After all, nothing awaited him except for the dull maid and a cramped room.

It was not that the Doctor lacked means. He could have lived in more comfortable circumstances had he wished. Yet somehow spending so much time alone, he lacked the incentive to provide for himself a stylish existence. He had almost grown to regard his patients' gifts of champagne or engravings as an embarrassment. He enjoyed suavity, or finesse, more when it could be admired in others.

When LeGrand turned his thoughts to his own existence, as he did from time to time, it would strike him with almost a pang of shame that his life was shabby and routine. He would be on the verge of considering why all freshness and enthusiasm had left him when he repeated to himself the salutary lessons that there was something degrading in self-pity. He vowed to live in the present, unencumbered by the maudlin feelings which rose out of day-dreaming about the past. These days he indulged too much in reverie and reflection on insoluble questions.

Besides, everybody had their troubles. He had even seen the tranquil atmosphere of the Grimauds' home disturbed. He had known the servants to be afraid to move from one room to another. For when Albert was born, some seven years ago, Mme Grimaud had been so ill that everyone had expected her to die.

The Doctor had delivered innumerable babies in his time yet he had never before known a woman whose labour had driven her to such hysteria. Grimaud himself apologized much later to the Doctor for the screams which had filled his own house. Then, as he was showing LeGrand to the front door, he glanced in the direction of the room where his wife now lay sleeping: his expression was taut with embarrassment and displeasure.

Later that week, while Mme Grimaud was still tired, the Doctor saw Albert's dark eyes staring steadily at him from the blue, silk-lined cot by his mother's bed. Looking up, LeGrand noticed Grimaud witnessing his wife's imitation of baby noises with distaste. Grimaud turned to his

son with a look of remote, even stern, consideration which
Albert, now gurgling and scowling, almost seemed to
return.

Later still, when there were panics over Albert's
health during which Mme Grimaud stood pressing a
handkerchief to her reddened eyes, fruitlessly looking to
her husband for comfort and saying that she could not bear
to lose her baby, the Doctor noticed Albert smiling. He
assured his mother that he was not suffering from whooping cough or tuberculosis, but warned her that he might
turn out to be musical: the infant lay gurgling like a small
drain.

In fact it was not so much for his musical talents that
LeGrand noticed Albert, although his mother tried to
interest him in the keyboard when he attempted to crawl
onto the grand piano wires. Nor did the Doctor especially
remember him for the occasion on which Albert, still no
more than a baby, had leant over from his mother's arms,
and pointed at LeGrand's birth-mark, asking:

'What's that?'

Rather, LeGrand had once had reason to visit their
house in the course of examining Mme Grimaud for the
first of her long series of internal complaints. Her husband
spoke to him afterwards in the drawing-room. Listening to
Grimaud's voice, constantly erupting through the con-
straints imposed by talking softly, the Doctor observed
the child framed in the doorway of another room. His
father, having first discussed the strange illness in what
the Doctor regarded as an oddly clinical manner, somehow turned to the subject of Egyptian Nationalism. It was
a theme to which he always seemed to be returning.

'Before we know where we are,' Grimaud said, his voice
growing louder, 'they'll be confiscating our property. If I
had my way I'd tear down that damn statue of Mohammed
Ali just to show them how far they can go.' LeGrand
laughed. 'No really. I'm serious. It's an obvious meeting
place. Anyway, the orthodox Mohammedans were against
it when it was first put up. That's why there's no in-
scription on it now.' Then LeGrand looked back at

Albert. 'You can't trust the British or French. What we need is someone to advance our interests here and now.'

The Doctor noticed the shifting form of the boy riding a rocking-horse.

On subsequent visits LeGrand found Albert in his father's study, lying on his stomach and turning the pages of a book which he had received for his seventh birthday, with a paint-box or crayons at his side. He would colour in the pictures of almost anything he was given, so that what had been a simple drawing might emerge as an illumination spilling onto the text. His mother, seeing how many books he had ruined, attempted to make him attend to his music lessons instead; but Grimaud, telling her that women should not meddle in education, supplied him with travel brochures. Thus Albert disfigured the burial masks of Pharaohs, while to the horse of Mohammed Ali he applied the same black and white patches as he daily observed on his own wooden steed.

'If he's interested in history,' his father once said as he sat with LeGrand watching Albert, 'I'll get him something worth painting.' The result was a book of great heroes, men who had made the world.

Albert applied his paints to great effect. Alexander and Caesar, Napoleon and Nero appeared more brilliant than ever before. None was immune from his brush. Sometimes, when M. Grimaud agreed to read out the text, Albert would find the inspiration for his colouring. Bonaparte's face was creased in an orange smile, for France, so the book said, revolved around Napoleon as it once had about *le roi soleil*; while a bilious Robespierre—'the sea-green incorruptible'—perfectly exemplified the description. Furthermore, when Grimaud put the volume down to tell Albert of the French Revolution, he unwittingly evoked a picture of Danton.

'Who's that?' LeGrand asked, looking at the red, pock-marked face.

'You,' was the boy's reply.

When the illustrations were complete M. Grimaud bought his son another book. It was less satisfactory, for being a work of recent history it contained fewer pictures. Indeed, from the Doctor's call one week to his visit the next Bismarck had been supplied with a purple moustache and beard, Louis Napoleon's cheeks had been rouged and his lips painted red, while Garibaldi's face now seemed like a highly baked biscuit. With these small additions the volume was abandoned: it clearly had no more to offer.

Or so it seemed. For M. Grimaud, not wishing to remain ignorant of the lessons which such an expensive book could teach, began reading it himself. Then drawing the boy away from the piano, to which his mother would tend to direct him each time she saw her husband picking up the volume, he paraphrased the fruits of his study for Albert's benefit.

LeGrand often sat in a comfortable arm-chair warming his brandy and glancing at Grimaud's highly polished shoes, as he learnt of what men of action could achieve.

'Look at what's been happening in Germany, and in Italy before that. Who'd have thought they'd have become great nations? They were just states with no idea where they were going. Yet it just needed leaders, men with enough determination. Don't you agree, Doctor?'

'Of course.'

'Where there's a will there's always a way.'

Albert appeared not to be listening. He was probably lying on the floor, only occasionally looking up as he detached the legs from a spider.

'Leave that alone. It's dirty,' his father said, giving him a tap on the hand.

Or else LeGrand would have been puffing at his cigar as Grimaud spoke of how important it was to be realistic. He released a cloud of bluish smoke as he heard that dreams were never enough.

'The Arabs live on nothing but dreams. Why try to change your life if you believe that every sparrow that falls, or every child that cries, is the will of Allah? What else do you have,' he turned a hand in the opaque atmosphere, 'but your empty dreams?'

'Haven't you forgotten Arabi though?'

'Bah! He'll never succeed. All his talk about freedom is an excuse for looting and violence. It's the easiest thing in the world to stir up stupid, ignorant people. They'll follow anyone.' He paused and studied LeGrand, considering his next sentence. 'We have our Arabs too, you know. They're not quite so blind or stupid, but they're just as bad in their own way. We have intellectuals. Look how many of the *Communards* were writers: and they hoped to abolish private property, exactly like Arabi. No, artists never improve anything. It's no use dreaming of destruction. That's just a form of weakness. It's not the way to change the world.'

The smoke drifted overhead for a moment only to become amorphous, then invisible, as the face of the gilt clock on the mantelpiece once again grew clear.

'Well, I think I must be going. I've got a long day ahead of me tomorrow.' But Grimaud, like Albert, ignored him, as the talk of great men continued.

'We live in an age of progress.' Albert had reestablished contact with the spider, which struggled about in a series of small circles now that it had been deprived of all but two neighbouring legs. 'We must go forward with it or else we shall be lost—leave it! I've told you before.' Albert looked up. 'Take Zionism, for example. At the moment it's just an idea, a dream. To go forward it needs a great man at the helm.'

'Well, why don't you go into politics since it interests you so much?' LeGrand asked, yawning.

'No. No. I'm not so young any more. Anyway I've got too many personal commitments. It needs someone at the start of their career, like my son perhaps,' he added, laughing. 'We need our own Napoleon to show Arabi and all the rest that we're here to stay.'

'I quite agree,' LeGrand said, looking deep into his brandy. As it happened, he had never understood how Grimaud could imagine that Jewish aspirations were identical with European interests. And remembering the Emperor's sojourn on St. Helena, he added: 'Of course Napoleon might not be the next example.'

Grimaud did not reply. There was the recurrent sound of the sea. Then, hearing the clock strike, he took out his watch, satisfied himself that it was correct and said:

'Well, it's late and young Albert here should have been in bed long ago. Anyway, you've got your tutor coming tomorrow, haven't you?'

'And I should have been getting along some time ago too.' When the Doctor was offered his hat and medical bag his host asked him again if Mme Grimaud's health was improving. As he gave his evasive reply LeGrand always considered how difficult it was to square Grimaud's testy treatment of his wife with such expressions of concern.

Grimaud followed the Doctor into the garden. There they stood still, drawing in deep breaths filled with scent from the dark flowers. Conversation lapsed until they turned to shake hands. And the Doctor would soon have left the lighted house and turned to the gates.

LeGrand noticed the glow of lamps inside as he arrived at the villa the evening after examining Grimaud's dead client. Glancing at the ragged blossoms of a flowering cactus, he almost believed that his present visit was similar to calls on other nights. Doubtless he had merely been summoned because of M. Grimaud's anxiety about his wife's condition.

Chapter 4

All day, since his return from certifying the corpse, LeGrand had been troubled by the feeling that he should contact M. Grimaud. If no one had told Grimaud of the murder perhaps he should; if someone had, it might be incumbent on him to offer consolation. Yet he simply spent his spare moments rocking in his chair, weakened by the heat, unable to decide what to do. By the evening he was still not sure if he should see Grimaud. Perhaps it might be as well to do nothing. After all, the Doctor had been exhausted by the night's events; he was too tired to cope with the distress caused by a murder. Nor could he be certain that his visit would not be interpreted as an unwanted intrusion. Sometimes he even felt that his appearance might be met with open hostility.

The Doctor was considering how cowardly he had always been in breaking bad news when a messenger interrupted his dinner. He wearily cut himself another slice of water-melon as the Arab asked him to visit M. Grimaud at once. Extracting the seeds individually, he waved the messenger on ahead with a trembling hand.

The servant was standing by a trellis, thick with jasmine, by the time LeGrand entered M. Grimaud's garden. The Doctor looked back from the porch to see if the Arab was still there, watching. He felt as if he were being observed long after the maid had closed the front door behind him.

LeGrand paused in the hallway, waiting to be summoned into the drawing-room. He had time to glance at a table containing framed photographs. In the wedding shots Grimaud seemed almost military; his shoulders were thrown back and he held his head high over his collar. Although his bride had smilingly taken his arm he seemed severe and remote: his expression was almost disdainful. By contrast, the Doctor found it hard not to think of Mme Grimaud as frail. Her features, protruding through so much embroidered silk, reminded him of the face which these days he usually saw surrounded by sheets and pillows.

There was a further photograph, probably taken two years before while they were on holiday by the Bosphorus. Mme Grimaud and two other ladies of about her age were sitting in long white dresses, holding parasols in a poppy field. She was hugging Albert as he sat in her lap. Yet the boy ignored her; he was looking gravely beyond the camera.

It must have been a slight rustle which turned the Doctor's attention away from the photograph to a doorway framing those same serious eyes. Albert was staring at LeGrand through the parting he had made in a bead curtain. For a moment the boy continued to look, standing in the fantastic shadows cast by an aspidistra in the lamplight. Then, when the Doctor nodded:

'Good evening,' and began walking over to Mme Grimaud's room, Albert let the coloured strands cascade over the navy blue shoulders of his sailor's outfit. He indicated his father's study instead.

As he approached the study LeGrand heard a low moaning. He looked back just as he put his fingers round the handle of the half open door. But Albert had disappeared, presumably to his bedroom. So the Doctor knocked hesitantly and then entered. He found M. Grimaud hunched up on a sofa.

'Oh God,' he was saying, 'Oh God.' The Doctor noticed that Grimaud's white frock coat, usually immaculate, was torn: one sleeve was covered in mud. His collar had sprung away from his throat. It was only attached by the back stud.

On seeing LeGrand enter Grimaud tried to get up, saying: 'Oh Doctor, Doctor.' He lurched forward, spilling the contents of the brandy balloon which he was holding.

LeGrand helped him back to the sofa. 'What on earth's happened?'

Grimaud answered by alternately repeating 'Oh God' and 'Oh Doctor'. He kept closing his eyes. His beard gleamed with amber drops of cognac each time his head and shoulders shivered with pain.

LeGrand, having accepted that he was unlikely to learn what had taken place for some minutes, allowed Grimaud's shudders time to subside. He sat on an arm of the sofa, a hand resting on his patient's shoulder. Before him he noticed a row of certificates attesting to Grimaud's competence in various spheres. There was even a framed letter from the French Ambassador acknowledging distinguished services to the French community.

As the Doctor began silently testing Grimaud's bones for fractures, moving the bruised limbs this way and that, he caught sight of the portrait of Grimaud's father which hung over the sofa. His black hair and dark clothes merged into a sombre background. Curious shapes, maybe a landscape or perhaps the irregular texture of the paint, seemed to loom large in the distance. It was only the mouth, LeGrand thought, which possessed any real colour. It was brilliant like the red faces which Albert often gave to his pictures of heroes. Even so, the thin lips were pressed together as tightly as the fingers which clasped a raised walking-stick.

Grimaud winced with pain. The Doctor released his patient's bruised foot and noticing how white he looked offered him a cigarette. LeGrand struck a match. Grimaud's face glowed for a moment. The flame lighted his pupils and brought a black sheen to his beard. Then the colour was extinguished and he fell back, surrounded by formless smoke.

LeGrand watched him without speaking. He was preparing what he would tell Grimaud about his physical condition when the moment seemed right. He could almost hear the matter-of-fact tone he used on such occasions:

'No broken bones, thank goodness. You're just suffering from a bit of shock—and, of course, a couple of bruises.'

Grimaud's expression no longer appeared strained. It was now vacant. Much to the Doctor's surprise his patient gave no sign of wanting to know the verdict on his health. He simply sat up and stubbed out his cigarette in an ashtray.

LeGrand concluded that the pain must have abated and, clearing his throat, began:

'Well, no broken bones, thank goodness. You're just——'

But Grimaud had already put a hand to his forehead. He interrupted with:

'I don't want you to say anything to Albert about this.'

'No. Of course not. I wouldn't.'

As the Doctor waited in solemn silence to hear what it

was that he had to keep secret, Grimaud leaned forward and belched. Then caressing his beard with the tips of his fingers, and gazing distantly at the brandy bottle, he began as if to himself:

'I was having an aperitif with a client near the Rue Rosette. I had a cognac,' he added. 'Just as we were going'—he waved a heavy hand—'down one of those side streets, you know,' he turned to LeGrand who nodded yet wore the perplexed look of one who was impatient for the point, 'he came up to us——'

'*Who* came up to you?'

'I recognized . . .' Grimaud screwed up his eyes, searching perhaps for the person's image, 'but I can't remember.' He opened the lids; once more he looked vacant; the tension had passed from his face.

'But you can't remember,' LeGrand prompted. By now the Doctor was finding it difficult to maintain the bland and considerate manner which was supposed to characterize members of his profession. For the strain of determining the assailant's identity, together with the shock of seeing a distinguished man like Grimaud reduced to childish incoherence, had unnerved him. Besides, the Doctor had to watch his words since he was not certain that Grimaud had heard of his client's murder: he did not wish him to learn of it unwittingly. Indeed he was not sure that it would be wise for him to be told at all in his present state—that was assuming the Doctor had the courage to tell him.

'I remember it was an Arab. He said something,' Grimaud went on, 'and then hit me.'

'What did you do?'

'It all happened so fast. I can't——' He gripped LeGrand's arm. 'I'm sorry. I'm embarrassing you.'

'No you're not,' the Doctor answered, moving in such a way as to disengage Grimaud's hand. Strong emotions, let alone hysteria, appalled him, especially in men. He thought them melodramatic. 'And what happened to your friend?' LeGrand asked wishing to avert further references to his distaste.

'My client. That's just it. I lost him.' Grimaud paused to consider what he had just said. 'The hotel says he hasn't come back yet.'

'You mean, when you . . .' LeGrand, more surprised by Grimaud's action than his ignorance, searched for the best word, 'went, he was left with the Arab?'

'Yes . . . I ran away.'

In the ensuing silence LeGrand, who felt he led a life independent of the conventional moral canon which extolled the virtues of bravery, did not dare to look at his patient's face. Grimaud's sense of shame had so charged the atmosphere that the Doctor found himself reproaching him for having deserted. His cowardice had left the wretched client to wander, terrified, through the Arab quarter, pursued by his eventual murderer; or else, having escaped, his companion had been beaten to death by another Egyptian in an alley near the harbour.

'Well, I shouldn't worry. I'm sure he's all right,' the Doctor remarked dully after a time. 'These Arabs never dare go too far. They're terrified of the police.'

'It's not that. It's having run away.'

'Come on now, you shouldn't get theatrical,' the Doctor said without premeditation. (He chose, as it happened, a rare occasion on which Grimaud seemed subdued.) 'Anyone would have done the same as you.'

'But imagine what it feels like to bring up a son who thinks you're not a man but a coward.' The Doctor looked first at his shoes and then at the carpet as he made his reply:

'I doubt if things are as bad as all that.'

Soon after LeGrand left the study. It was a relief to pass from the buzzing lamp, in whose constant glare Grimaud, more thoughtfully now, was still slouched, into the candle-lit hall. Crossing the marble floor LeGrand noticed four squares of even paler light. He was able to see clouds floating across the moon as he looked past the open door to the window of Albert's room.

Glancing down, LeGrand observed a pyramid built out of toy bricks. Around its base, set in a tray of sand, toy soldiers maintained its position; they were fighting off Arab marauders. LeGrand did not understand, as he moved nearer, how these miniatures stood up to the adults entering and leaving the room all day. And how was it that the door did not slam on the fortress? Perhaps Albert was always vigilant. Maybe he was lying awake, anticipating exactly where the Doctor would step next. LeGrand wondered, just as he awoke to the eerie possibility of being watched by those unflinching eyes, if the boy was also aware of the conversation with his father. If so, and the young man was at least conscious of Grimaud's weakened state, did he realize what it implied? Was the Doctor, indeed, sure that he himself fully grasped what the interview meant? As LeGrand continued speculating on the possible effects of the evening's events on Albert he followed the intricate paths traced by a pair of mosquitoes through the toy fort. They droned on, endlessly intertwining and separating over the parapets. At last they drew together no more. They were lost in the darkness.

PART II
A Year Later

An Arab Funeral

Chapter 5

It seemed that the singing would never stop. The mourners, all men, repeated their chant again and again as they carried the bodies to Chatby. Only the throb of their voices, like a magnified drone of flies, sounded through shadowless squares where camels sat dazed by the heat.

Down the long, dusty streets of Alexandria the Arab funeral made its slow way. It passed along avenues of palm trees, continually swelling its numbers. Silent Europeans, peering from their verandas, looked over the heads of bystanders, not daring to go out. Below them the line of expressionless faces, distorted by the intervening light, bore off shrouded corpses with a persistent sound.

The bodies swayed rhythmically on the glistening shoulders of Negroes. They headed the procession through the motionless city. Their destination was still far off in the distance: the cemetery appeared like an outskirt of the desert.

Each Arab trod on apparently indifferent to the fiery sea to his right. Not one looked beyond his own footsteps or the hem of the *gallabiya* before him. With their eyes hooded and lowered, Pierre LeGrand imagined that they were in a trance.

The Doctor had been watching the cortège for nearly ten minutes now; for his tram, with its reins in Arab hands, had deferentially stopped and allowed the procession to cross its path. LeGrand's first impulse had been to rebuke the driver and leave the scorching cage. He had seen so many outrages committed against acquaintances and patients in the year which had elapsed since the murder of M. Grimaud's client, that he had little sympathy for the half-dozen Egyptians killed in yesterday's riot. Besides it seemed that every time he returned from visiting patients in Ramleh, as he was doing from the Grimauds' house this afternoon, the vehicle encountered some infuriating obstacle: a herd of goats idling on the road; a child squatting and relieving itself; and now a funeral. Yet recalling the violence of the previous day, and searching in vain for a fellow-European face, he thought it best not to draw attention to himself. Wearily, he reconciled himself to waiting.

Soon all the Doctor's impatience had passed. Sitting in the strong, mid-afternoon light, he was unconscious of any particular feeling or mood. There were only his senses: and even LeGrand's awareness of the procession shifted from his vision of each Arab marching past, to a drowsy image of white winding endlessly on. Each time he re-awakened from a doze, never longer than a few seconds, or at the most a minute, he seemed to carry some part of his simpler, yet sterner, perception of the funeral from his reverie. Thus it was that he now imagined the mourners to be entranced. The present appeared at once more remote and more potent, freed, as in dreams, from the confinements of time.

LeGrand frequently found that events in his life felt unreal in this way as they were happening; and fantasies acquired the impact of life. While he wrote out a pre-scription or hummed a tune he would pause and ask himself:

'Am I really here? Is this now? Am I sure I exist?' Then the everyday things—the rocking-chair, his front collar stud, his scarred cheek—would grow unaccountably strange. And the invisible barrier between himself and others, or the past and the present, might lift. Per-sonalities, times, threatened to merge in dark chaos;

dreams seemed entirely lifelike, and his life like a dream.

LeGrand recalled having felt adrift in this way during yesterday's rioting. He remembered that he had been drinking coffee on the Boulevard Ramleh when a youth ran towards him with taut lips, brandishing a chair. LeGrand managed to hide in the lavatory at the back of a café. All he could think of as he waited, stifled by the earthen pit, were yellow teeth, gritted as they approached him. He could hear screams outside. Some seemed to come from the café, others from the road, and still more from the streets beyond. Sometimes he heard a whistle. Once there was a low rumble: it could have been the vibrations of a gun. Yet as LeGrand stood, overcome by the stench, and frenzied by the constant collision of flies, the noises seemed to solidify and gather. Almost fainting, he gained the impression that they were issuing from behind gigantic, yellow teeth.

When, at last, LeGrand opened the lavatory door he saw an Arab leaning against the opposite wall. The Doctor drew back, but then realized that the man was incapable of seeing him. He was bending forward, his front teeth mere shattered stumps, vomiting blood into the darkness.

Leaving the café, LeGrand found the light blinding. The noise of street fighting deafened him. He was alarmed by shrieking nearby. He knew that he must return to his flat immediately, for the situation could not be more dangerous; yet all he could see were luminous specks. They drifted vaguely before him on a watery film.

In the avenue the translucent particles turned to fire. LeGrand blinked, shading his eyes with a hand, but the specks continued their leisurely movement across his eyelids. Desperate to regain his full sight he swung back to the darkness. He carried the incandescence with him. Then his fingers touched cloth. He started back. He had seen the face of a blind beggar.

Sitting in the tram now, almost exactly a day later, the Doctor remembered the beggar moaning for money: LeGrand was still listening to the funeral chant. He closed his eyes and longed for silence. He could hardly believe that it had existed in Ramleh less than an hour before.

All had been quiet by the Grimauds' house. The eucalyptus trees and cypresses had been motionless in the surrounding gardens. The brilliant sky deprived the flowers, descending tier by tier, of their depth; and the bluish-green grass, curving away to the sea, bore no prints except for the light tracks of horses.

LeGrand recalled, as he turned away from the mourners, the amazement which he had felt at the pacific sensations overcoming him during the riot. Aquamarine palm leaves had quivered in a wash of light: and the two minarets of the Mohammed Ali Mosque shimmered over the city.

While the Doctor was standing outside the café, stupefied, he noticed a barber running towards him. The Arab screamed, holding a cut-throat razor, with his other hand full of lather. As LeGrand ran backwards, he hit his head against a fibrous trunk. He went on running despite the pain.

He ran right across the Boulevard. The light was blinding. He saw the elongated, white forms of Arabs overturning a tram. One of its passengers, a Rabbi, was staring into the sun, as he tottered away from the vehicle. His black arm hung at a distorted angle. LeGrand thought of helping him. Despite his tired legs he moved on.

The Doctor found street urchins throwing lumps of earth and old timber through his flat windows as he reached the road where he lived. He stood for a moment hearing himself shout. The boys turned round. One swore in Arabic. LeGrand saw the youth move closer. Suddenly there was a terrible pain in his arm. A piece of brick lay at his feet.

The Doctor's entire shoulder began throbbing as he ran on. He murmured his destination:

'Daniel Benchimol's house near Mohammed Ali Square.' It was repeated like a heartbeat.

In the distance cannon thudded. They made the buildings vibrate. Each blast seemed to coincide with an even more intense wave of pain. LeGrand stopped, leaning against an alley wall, thinking his lungs would explode. No sooner had he taken out a handkerchief to wipe his face than he heard cheers overriding the rifle shots.

The shouting went on for minutes without end. The clapping and singing drew everyone who was not already in the square through its adjoining passages. LeGrand tried to hide in a doorway, but the sheer mass of Arabs drove him from the recess and carried him out into the main body of people.

The crowd pushed and shouted, scarcely able to move in the alley. Only the bright glow of the Square seemed to summon it on. LeGrand struggled, surrounded by dark faces. Shoulders wheeled: eyes glistened: there was the flashing of gold teeth.

An old woman stood writhing with her head back. Her toothless mouth shrieked up to the stone passageway ceiling. No sooner had LeGrand looked towards her than he felt a hand tip off his hat. It bobbed about for a moment. Watching it disappear through the turbulent surface, he looked back and found that the old woman had gone.

By now the cheering was growing more and more rhythmical. The dense column of people in the alley answered the shouting in the Square with its cries.

'Bloody savages!' the Doctor called when somebody knocked his bruised shoulder. An angry Arab spat on his scarred cheek. LeGrand tried to pull out a hand with which to wipe off the spittle but, unable to unlock his arm, he felt the saliva roll down his face and run into the sweat on his neck.

Finally they surged into the brilliant light. Cheers reverberated through the buildings which made up the Square. Egyptians were firing triumphal shots from the roofs of government offices. As they were pushed nearer to the centre LeGrand saw someone clinging to the statue of Mohammed Ali.

The crowd roared with delight at the young man who joined the Arab leader on horseback. The youth laughed, waving, as though he were scattering flowers, with a majestic turn of the wrist. Yet he was unaware of the other boys who had just climbed onto the plinth. They pulled him from the shiny saddle and mounted the steed among cheers identical with those which had greeted their predecessor. They too were dislodged in a matter of moments: and the crowd had gone on to acclaim any group which had succeeded in occupying the narrow space of burning metal even if only for a short time.

LeGrand remembered, as the funeral procession continued chanting, how the cheering had stopped and started at almost regular intervals. Watching the shrouded corpses swinging on Negro shoulders, he recalled the predictable way in which each combination of riders had been supplanted on the animal's back. A man had suddenly climbed onto the statue. The applause had risen to a crescendo. The individual stood with a hand on the saddle, a small figure wearing a *gallabiya*. LeGrand could not see the face clearly, but thought that it might have been Arabi Pacha.

Looking now at the interminable line of white-clad mourners, the Doctor felt that the person's features could have belonged to any of these heads. He yawned and found that all the physiognomies had began to coalesce in his mind's eye. In an instant LeGrand was breathing heavily: his head fell onto his chest.

The strange imagined mask began to encompass yesterday's faces as well as today's. It hovered for a while over the past and the present, and indifferent to either it floated capriciously away.

Chapter 6

Albert Grimaud was watching the cortège advancing towards Chatby from a café in Mohammed Ali Square. The boy imagined that the front of the procession had already reached the Boulevard Ramleh as he added a fifth spoonful of sugar to his glass of lemonade. Having stirred it five times, once for each spoonful, he sipped and observed the mourners passing the equestrian statue.

Albert found that if he moved his head and shoulders slightly to the left he could see the funeral through the leaves of a nearby acacia tree. Naturally this funeral could not be the same funeral as he saw when he sat up straight, or so he decided. So what he was seeing now must be another part of the procession, perhaps the first mourners entering the Boulevard Ramleh. The statue was really a tram that had been stopped.

Soon he noticed that the plinth was dripping green. Albert remembered that green was the colour of animal blood. Accordingly the vehicle was converted back into a horse. He sat up and found himself back in Mohammed Ali Square.

Besides, green was the colour with which he had painted a cavalry charge hundreds of years back, long before he had reached his considerable age of eight. And Albert had just decided that when he looked at the Square without the intermediary of an acacia tree he was really living all that time ago.

'Why are the horses green?' he remembered his great-aunt Stella had inquired. (She was naturally asking him *now*.) Albert was sitting on his bedroom floor mixing yellow paint with blue, just as his father had recently shown him. He looked up, but did not tell her his secret. He and his father, for whom the picture was being painted, were the only people in the whole world who knew that animals had green blood—except horses; but then they had not been able to speak to anybody but Albert.

A mourner brushed by the statue. He wore pink and white striped pyjamas and held a bamboo cane. Albert had often seen Arabs dressed in this way; he had also noticed European gentlemen wearing dust-coats, which looked like nightshirts, over their suits on trains. But if people wore nightclothes during the day, he had asked his father —his vision, still unimpaired by the acacia tree, continued miraculously to up-date the past—what did they wear at night?

Albert could not remember M. Grimaud's answer. He tried but only recalled having felt bewildered when everyone had laughed. The game he was now playing was clearly losing its magic. Anyway he never liked doing one thing for too long. He would forget about the past, and invent something else.

Yet, quite unsolicited, an image from that same part of his childhood crossed his mind: he himself was wearing a white nightshirt and his father called him:

'My little white man.'

M. Grimaud often played with Albert for a while before bedtime. Placing his son on the toy horse he rocked him faster and faster. He would laugh and, putting an arm round the boy's waist, steady the animal as Albert screamed with delight.

What Albert could not understand, as he looked at a further Arab crossing the Square in pyjamas and then down at his own sailor suit, was why he was always forbidden to leave his room in a nightshirt when there were visitors.

'The Egyptians do.'

'But they're different,' he was told.

Albert could remember an occasion—again, it had been all that time ago, before his fifth birthday even, when he had been very young—when he had been sent to bed early; for Dr. LeGrand was coming to visit his mother. Albert was sitting on his horse, rocking in the doorway. He thought that they would never stop talking.

'Go to bed,' his father said immediately after the Doctor had left. 'We can't have you running around like that.'

'But I'm not running. I'm riding.'

'Don't argue. Now do as I say and get into bed.'

Albert wondered, sipping his lemonade, if adults could help being so peculiar. His father had rarely tried to answer questions directly. The most obvious things never seemed to occur to him.

'Papa. Why has the Doctor got raspberry jam on his face?' Albert had inquired on the same evening.

'Don't be rude!' M. Grimaud gave his son a playful tap on the hand. 'He's a very nice man and he's known us since before you were born.'

Albert's father tickled his cheek as he bent over to kiss him:

'Good night.' M. Grimaud's beard smelt of cologne and cigar smoke.

Sometimes Albert considered that adults were another breed altogether. He could not see how he himself would ever grow into one of them. Perhaps they were like horses, with their own language. Certainly Albert knew that he could barely understand them when they spoke to one another at the table. Their conversation in the drawing-room, at least if he heard it from his bed, sounded like the droning of flies interrupted by barking.

He recalled how they seemed to go on talking in the study for ever the night that his father had been attacked. It had happened a whole year ago, though it did not seem so remote as his other memories. Yet he could remember keeping completely still, not daring to climb out of bed as he usually did. All the grown-ups—his father, his mother, Dr. LeGrand, even the servants—became so serious all of a sudden that Albert was no longer sure if he should behave as normal. He had even felt awkward lying without moving.

Albert was nervous now too. The sound of the procession continued, the sugary lemonade burned his throat, it was so hot that he could scarcely breathe, and he knew that his father would doubtless be furious when he discovered that his son had left the house without asking permission. Not that his father would have allowed him to go if he had asked, for M. Grimaud had grown violently moody recently. He disapproved of people or habits for no reasons which Albert could understand. And his opinions, like his temper, were so subject to whimsy that Albert had learned to be secretive rather than to say anything which might conceivably excite disapproval. Better still, he avoided his father.

Albert would have liked to avoid thinking about him

now, as he watched the funeral procession, but he could not prevent himself from anticipating his father's anger. Nor, either with or without the help of acacia leaves, could he stop wondering why certain things which he had once taken as a matter of course, such as kissing his father or entering his study, had come to seem tacitly unacceptable. These were matters about which he would never dream of asking.

Even more persistent in his mind was an image from that same night, the evening on which his father had been attacked. It was an impression which had overcome him from time to time, and whose dark eeriness, even when he was sitting in the intense sunlight as now, he found impossible to forget.

Albert had been listening to the sounds of the conversation when he realized that there had been silence for some moments. Sitting up in bed to see if there was light beneath the study door, he suddenly held his breath and kept still. There was somebody watching him. Albert could not remember how long the figure had stayed. It seemed for ever. He could only recall a man turning towards the fort and knocking over a toy soldier with his shoe on leaving.

Later Albert went to replace the fallen piece.

'What are you doing?' his father demanded in a low, toneless voice as he emerged from the study.

'Someone's knocked over my soldiers,' Albert said accusingly. His father entered and sprawled out awkwardly on the floor next to him. Albert saw that his eyes were red and thought he must have been crying.

'Well, don't look at me like that.' Albert had never seen his father cry before. 'It must have been LeGrand. The trouble with him is that he's too interested in other people's business.' Albert felt disturbed in some incoherent way both by his father's proximity—there was the smell of brandy on his breath—and seeing him so physically weak. 'He's never made anything of himself. He's just a pathetic old woman.' Albert had moved away, wishing that his father would simply go. And now, as he watched the funeral procession, remembering quite how broken his father had appeared, Albert felt afraid again. His fear grew into momentary panic, keener than his terror on recalling the stranger by his bed or reflecting on M. Grimaud's anger.

Albert's father had paused and then taken a flag, made out of a matchstick and painted paper, from the fort. He drew its head along a crack between two tiles to light his cigar.

'You've ruined my flag,' Albert said.

'Oh, don't you start too. You're becoming as bad as your mother.' Then his father had grown silent and still.

Albert remembered having seen M. Grimaud's face light up as the paper had turned to flame. The boy had thought he looked so distant, so strange, that he had wondered if he was really his father. Grimaud's eyes became glistening hollows. Soon they were obscured by smoke. But Albert had pretended to be invisible by then. Recalling Grimaud's fingers holding smouldering tatters Albert imagined himself watching the funeral unobserved.

Chapter 7

LeGrand shifted drowsily in his tram seat. The sky was turning to red. The setting sun enflamed a low-lying column of cloud. It ruddied the sea and coloured the shoulders of mourners.

The Doctor, trying to shake off his weariness, consulted a pocket watch. He shook his head at the hour and deplored the disruption of his routine. Yet he found it difficult to concentrate on the problem of how to get back to the flat in time for evening surgery. Pictures of Arabs carrying firebrands, as they had done in yesterday's riot, crossed his mind.

Egyptians had left Mohammed Ali Square once the speeches had ended. Lighting bales of cotton dragged out of nearby warehouses, they set them at the doors of government buildings and the entrances of European shops.

LeGrand passed an Arab on crutches who was tying the legs of stray cats together and casting them, live, into a fire. A woman shrieked in Greek and threw lumps of dried earth from the geranium pots set on her second-floor veranda. Her ragged poodle, that had somehow strayed from the block of flats into the street, was joined by a piece of rag to another consignment of cats. The animals snarled as they were doused in paraffin. Their cries rose, becoming more frenetic as the cripple took his crutch, carefully used its end to lift the binding cord, and let them slide into the furnace of cotton.

LeGrand turned into another road. So many bales were alight that the air seemed to quiver above them; it almost melted into the smoke. As the Doctor passed into the Rue Rosette he found the heat even more intense. Timber and further bales of cotton crackled down the centre of the road: windows and glass shop fronts cracked with the flames.

By the time he thought of turning back LeGrand saw what looked like a blazing barricade stretching across the street. As he drew nearer his eyes kept closing. Then, standing almost directly in front of the bales, they suddenly opened wide. He stared, transfixed by the flames.

LeGrand had suffered from a headache all night. His eyes smarted so much that he bathed them again and again in a solution. They hurt now, again as he looked at the sunset from the tram.

Of course, the Doctor realized that he was hardly a casualty. Those who had really suffered were men like Solomon Grimaud. Most of the cotton which the rioters had used for yesterday's bonfires had been rifled from his warehouses. His offices in the Rue Rosette were entirely burned out. The gold sign:

GRIMAUD

was now charred.

AN ARAB FUNERAL

LeGrand had walked down the street earlier this afternoon, hours previous to the funeral procession. It was
shortly before making Mme Grimaud one of his regular
visits. He saw Arabs ambling along, apparently indifferent
to the metal characters which lay shattered on the pave-
ment. Some were just curious enough to peer at the skeleton of black brick. In Ramleh too, perhaps an hour or so
later, the air seemed untroubled and clear. Walls looked
as if they had only recently been whitewashed. A bee
hovered uneasily over the long stamen of a giant flower,
so loaded with pollen that it could hardly raise its yellowed
legs.

Inside the villa there was no sun. The blinds were still
drawn; cupboards with glass fronts full of silver, and
ritual crockery used only once a year, had been pushed
against the drawing-room windows as if in defence. For
some time the Doctor encountered nobody except the maid
who had opened the door. He was idly watching dust
dancing up and down the few cracks of light. Each speck
faded into the blue velvet folds of the curtains. Somewhere
in the silence there was a regular noise. It could have been
a clock, or the movement of pendant glass on a chandelier.

Looking at the Arab mourners now passing into the near
darkness, LeGrand again realized how odd the situation
had been. From the moment that he made out M.
Grimaud's form slumped over a chair in the study he understood that Mme Grimaud was not his only, still less his
most urgent, patient.

Grimaud's chin had fallen onto his chest and the beard
was growing beyond the places where he usually shaved.
His forehead was smeared with soot. He did not look up
when the Doctor first called to him. It was only when
LeGrand touched him on the shoulder that he opened his
bloodshot eyes and spoke. He asked in a voice empty of all
expression or emotion:

'What's the time?'

As the Doctor pulled out his watch he felt, as he
occasionally did, that the events of the present were not
happening for the first time. LeGrand's actions, his

thoughts, the whole morbid atmosphere seemed to have enjoyed a previous existence. Perhaps it was the attempt to bring some identical situation to mind that made M. Grimaud's condition appear unreal. The Doctor was only able to concentrate on his patient by scrutinizing him for signs of physical injury.

Grimaud was not even bruised. He was weary, still, and rather quiet. He had been the same shortly after learning of his client's murder. On both occasions, LeGrand reflected in the tram, Grimaud had merely sat snapping matchsticks: and whereas the Doctor had waited for him to mention the death, or this afternoon his financial losses, he began in a subdued voice to speak of his son.

'I would like my son to travel. I think he should see something of the world. Human nature can never be learnt too young.' Grimaud had paused between each comment as they descended the garden, tier by tier, only twelve months ago. 'I want him to know how to cope with situations. Be independent. If necessary be alone.' He put a hand on LeGrand's shoulder and stood still, staring into the darkness. 'A man should not be womanish or weak.' There was the heavy fragrance of flowers. 'His mother has too much influence with him, you know.' Grimaud looked into the Doctor's eyes confidentially. Dropping his arm from LeGrand's back he added almost gruffly: 'I'm sure that he'll have the resources to stand up on his own.'

This afternoon, LeGrand recalled, watching the last mourners crossing the tram's path, Grimaud had not been dressed immaculately as before; but he was, at least to begin with, just as polite. The Doctor accepted his invitation to a cognac, though he rarely drank during the day. They were watched by a shadowy Napoleon brooding in the corner cabinet where the brandy bottle stood.

'Have you seen Albert?' M. Grimaud asked vaguely. He was staring at the spectrum elicited from his glass by a stray ray of light. 'He could have a brilliant future if he would only stop going his own way and learn to do as he's told.'

AN ARAB FUNERAL

The Doctor was relieved that Grimaud did not pause for an answer since he had scarcely listened to the question. LeGrand had been realizing what appeared obvious now he had seen it, that this situation—the study, the darkness, Grimaud's misfortune—was not only identical with the situation of a year ago, but also that it was the sole context in which he could think of his patient. M. Grimaud's past and present somehow coalesced in the Doctor's mind in this maudlin image. LeGrand could not remember, or even believe in, the successful Grimaud who had once seemed self-assured and cavalier.

By now Grimaud was standing in the middle of the room. His vision seemed to penetrate beyond the Empire bookcase set before the window. Then, focusing his sight on the leather-bound volumes, he reached for an edition of Plutarch's *Lives*. It stood between Rashi's Commentaries and the works of Maimonides. After scanning a few pages he gazed, with eyes as basilisk-like as marble, at a small chink of light.

The Doctor, having remembered what the present had reminded him of, felt momentarily less abstracted. Yet his patient's strange expression once more made the situation seem unreal. Grimaud's politeness evolved into an unnerving way of talking:

'What a terrible thing to see a vision brought down by barbaric fools.'

His speech scarcely resembled anything that the Doctor had heard him say before. Grimaud spoke as if with somebody else's voice.

'It's all over now. Everything I fought for has gone! I'll only ask them one question: was it for myself that I built an Empire?' His eyes were large, heavy, and red. 'I gave them life. I inspired them.' LeGrand never fully grasped what he was saying. He merely glimpsed it and imagined that he was supposed to understand. 'Then they tried to destroy everything. They deserted me. Don't go!' he implored the Doctor when, unable to continue listening, LeGrand got up on the pretext of visiting Mme Grimaud. 'Everyone's deserting me now—even my own son!'

The Doctor sat down again and heard more of the self-willed Albert; but soon M. Grimaud had been conversing entirely with himself.

Grimaud's complaint, the Doctor now reflected in the dark tram, belonged to a particularly unsavoury group of illnesses —not that LeGrand considered that a man of Grimaud's impeccable family and background was ever likely to go, well, mad. Nevertheless the Doctor preferred not to probe into mental disorders, be they senility, the kind of frenzy you could see in almost any street of the Arab quarter, or, as in M. Grimaud's case, melancholia and the effects of great strain. After all, if you turned over a stone, LeGrand thought, and were bitten by a snake you had nobody but yourself to blame. Those few specialists like Professor Valence, the Frenchman who ran an experimental clinic in what was virtually desert, were considered quacks by the entire medical profession. Valence himself, so LeGrand had heard, may have been inspired but he was certainly very odd.

M. Grimaud would undoubtedly recover. He had proved wonderfully resilient in the weeks after he had been attacked. Yet no matter how light or severe his infirmity, his conversation had manifested the one defect which LeGrand knew was a characteristic of most forms of mental unbalance: an imperfect sense of reality and time. Grimaud had spoken as though in a dream. He glided over immediate issues—his wife, his health, his business—pursuing chance themes at tangents, ignoring visitors and his surroundings, behaving as if the scorching afternoon had been night . . .

LeGrand was suddenly thrown forward in his seat. The tram horses whinnied as they drew off. He could scarcely believe that the jerky motion was real after such a delay. The sounds of the wheels and the harnesses seemed strange in the quiet evening. And looking into the darkness the Doctor still caught himself thinking of the events of the preceding hours and days.

Chapter 8

Albert could see torches returning from the cemetery at Chatby. The first firebrands were already emerging from the streets which led into the Square. They flickered between the bronze legs of Mohammed Ali's horse.

Albert imagined that the mourners were really little men climbing out of the animal's belly, like the soldiers in a bedtime story which M. Grimaud had once told long ago. (The wooden steed had been a present, he remembered, similar to the painting of a cavalry charge which he had given to his father.) The invaders ran unseen, except by Albert, among the high buildings. A far-off ship's lantern, melting into the sea, answered signals from a tower. Soon armies would have landed; the whole city would be blazing; entire households might be slaughtered together with their heads. Then, after smouldering all night, everything would have turned to grey cinders, like expanses of sand in the dawn.

The victors, of whom Albert had now naturally become chief, would ride through the silent noon streets, lined with ruined buildings. His polished helmet, continually catching the sun as he rose and fell smartly in the saddle, returned shafts of blinding light; but the few surviving inhabitants would be hiding in dark crannies and shelters.

Albert blinked as the torches continued to flicker around Mohammed Ali's statue. They looked like glowing insects in the night. The mourners' voices sounded disembodied. On the cobbled square there were footfalls, noises made with invisible heels.

Albert remembered that everything had felt so strange when he had worn a giant mask at a Mardi Gras carnival in Cairo years before, that it seemed to be happening by magic. His father, still wearing the red, white, and blue decoration which the French Ambassador had pinned to the lapel of his morning coat only hours earlier, lowered the papier-mâché head onto his son's shoulders. Albert found it hot and dark in there; it smelt of paint and glue.

Manipulating the enormous eyes and mouth the boy discovered that he could imagine the outside world away. The laughter of the other masked children, running through the Embassy gardens, sounded distant and insubstantial; and the applause of parents, of whom several had been decorated at the same time as his father, was lost in the splashing of fountains and the slight roar of a miniature waterfall.

Albert recalled that all the heads had been caricatures of national figures. In the early evening, before the banquet in honour of the new *chevaliers* and France, the children were invited to assemble in a long, candle-lit room to make the acquaintances of cardboard monarchs: the Emperor Charlemagne, Catherine de Medici, Henry IV, and Louis XIV. Albert could not remember which ruler he had lifted from the tailor's dummy; he had an idea that it was Napoleon—or maybe Bonaparte.

'I think you should take it off, darling, or else you'll suffocate,' he heard his mother say. There was the sound of her fan. But since Albert, who had been roaming the garden in the head for some time now, realized that the world did not exist, he was compelled to ignore Mme Grimaud's plea. 'Albert! Come back! Why are you such a naughty boy?' He tramped away from her, giant-like, through the primeval chaos of an ornamental pool.

On his return to civilization—minus the shoe in which he had attempted, and failed, to catch a goldfish which had once been a falling star—Albert heard his mother urgently discussing her 'baby's' safety with M. Grimaud.

'For God's sake stop . . .' His father tried to quell her mounting anxiety but broke off in the middle of his sentence for fear of attracting the attention of the other guests. 'Ah! What did I tell you? Here comes the little rascal.' His father laughed and puffed at his cigar as if to blow away his wife's nervousness as easily as smoke. He went to meet his bedraggled son, who was walking with one bare foot across the lawn.

Albert made no effort to explain what his mother called his 'wicked disobedience' on the way back to the hotel. He simply sat—bathed, combed, and spanked—his legs dangling over the edge of the double bed, sighing as he watched his parents laboriously dress for the banquet. His father must have tied his white tie at least three times. It always seemed to go wrong when he turned from the mirror to talk.

'You *must* learn to leave the child alone, Ivette. It's normal for boys to run a bit wild.' Then, looping an end behind the front bow M. Grimaud went on: 'He must learn to be independent and stand on his own feet. How, in God's name, is he going to develop any will of his own if all he sees are pianos and tears?' He was fixing the clasp on the back of his wife's necklace when he added more quietly, as if pleading: 'Look at him now. He's terribly secretive and strange.' Yet hardly turning to Albert, who was still swinging his feet against the bed, he continued: 'If our boy is going to grow up to be anything in this world we mustn't be over-anxious or keep making concessions to him. It'll only make him weak. I'm sure you understand, don't you, darling?' He leant over and kissed her lightly on the shoulder.

A little later Mme Grimaud entered Albert's bedroom to say:

'Good night,' before leaving for the Embassy. She smelt of lily of the valley. 'Did you enjoy the carnival, darling?' she asked softly. Albert did not answer. He was pretending to be asleep.

'Leave him,' his father whispered at the door. 'I'm not surprised the poor boy's exhausted. Besides, we're going to be late.'

His mother kissed the motionless face and pulled bedclothes around Albert's shoulders. He could see the sheen of her dress through his half opened eyes. White fingers —everybody had remarked on Mme Grimaud's beautifully fair complexion—joined his father's robust hand in the hallway. There was darkness, and then total silence.

A minute later Albert yearned to call his parents back. He was afraid to sleep in the room alone. Yet by now they had probably reached the hotel foyer: and now they were sitting in their carriage. He followed their progress all the way to the banqueting hall. Albert imagined their grand entrance from the bottom of his bed. There at least, head first, he knew he would be safe. Perhaps his parents would never be able to find him in the morning . . .

Everything in the Square, it seemed to Albert, had finally lost its outline. Mourners carrying torches were deserting Mohammed Ali's statue for their homes. The shadow patterns cast by acacia leaves had long since faded from the cobbles. Even the solid mass of branches had dissolved into the night.

Albert knew that his father would also be sitting in pitch darkness.

'Albert!' he would be calling. 'Albert! Why don't you come when you're told?' M. Grimaud might go on to add to himself, as he had done for some months now: 'The trouble with that boy is that he's got too much will of his own.'

Recently Albert could hardly bear to enter the study. It smelt of oil lamps and hot leather. Although the sun was excluded by a blind, light showed through the faded areas of fabric. At noon, when the heat was most intense, the material gave off a red glow.

'Now sit down on the sofa next to me and tell me what you're doing with your Arabic tutor. Does he ever talk about politics?' Albert could never concentrate on his father's questions. He would sit on his hands, unable to think of anything except the tall sheikh who always arranged their next lesson for the late afternoon in the hope of being invited to stay on for dinner. 'What's he been saying about Arabi, for instance?' When the Arab opened his lips Albert wondered if he might conceivably be blinded, for his teacher's copious gold teeth, invariably closing over a spoonful of marmalade taken from the decorated jar of which it was customary to eat no more than a few mouthfuls, caught and reflected the sun.

In the last few days M. Grimaud had started shouting but not only when his son failed to provide answers. For Albert need not have been anywhere near his father to provoke some frightening outburst, though how or why he had done so the boy could never understand.

'To think of the money I've spent on your education! Just look at the result! If you'd work half as hard as I've had to you'd be a success.' Albert had watched Grimaud, unkempt and unshaven, from behind the banister rails. 'But you'll never make a success. You're a disgrace to the family. You're so *weak*!' Albert saw his father shout the word with all the strength in his once powerful body. Grimaud had begun pacing up and down behind the bars . . .

As Albert left the café a waiter, holding the lemonade glass on a saucer with one hand, twisted the final chair onto its table with the other. Realizing quite how late it must be Albert began walking through the Square as fast as he could.

Surely it had been even later on the previous evening when he had been woken by his father's shouting. The worst had undoubtedly happened then. It might almost have passed ten o'clock for Albert was certain that he had been sleeping for hours.

'How *could* you help? You *couldn't* understand.' The boy soon realized that Grimaud was not referring to him. 'If you were a real wife——' His voice grew more high-pitched and nervous.

'But Solomon, tell me what's happened,' she interrupted weakly. 'Can things really be so bad? If only you would forget the firm sometimes! You've already sacrificed our health and happiness to it. Must you always consider business before your wife and child?'

Albert sat up in bed; then creeping over to the door he looked into his mother's room. Her fingers, constantly fidgeting, were swollen and blue. Her hair, dulled from chestnut into an indistinct brown, perhaps by the lamplight, lay loosely on the pillow. Tortoise-shell slides had been abandoned long ago to her dressing table.

While Grimaud continued to make his savagely disdainful remarks, many of which the boy could neither hear nor understand, Albert tried to pretend that he was witnessing a play. The shadowy figures, the rising voices were on stage: they were unreal. Albert remembered playing a father in a sketch which he had once put on in the garden with some young friends . . .

'You don't know they've been rioting! You don't know what a mess the business is in, do you? And what's more, you don't even care! You've just been lying there, useless, for God knows how long!' (Albert had quite forgotten that this was drama. Although he knew that his father was not shouting at him he was hiding behind the door.)

'Your illness has cost me a fortune. You could get up and *do* something if you really wanted to! You've done your best to spoil Albert and set him against me. And now you think you'll relax while my business is ruined!' There was a pause. 'But you won't! Get up!' Grimaud was shouting furiously. 'Get up, I say!'

'No—No—Ah . . . !'

Albert noticed muffled sounds, like moaning: his mother might have been talking, but he thought he heard sobs.

'Get up!' Grimaud's eyes were wide open. His grimy face trembled. Veins stood out on his temples and neck. 'Get up! You're as bad as all the rest of them. You want to destroy me, pull me do-w-n!'

'A-h-h-h!' He suddenly clenched his teeth, and gripping her hands he slapped her across the face. Albert heard his father shriek over the near-hysterical crying:

'Stop it! I hate you! I hope you die!'

There was silence in the house soon afterwards. Albert's mother stopped crying, but he had not been able to sleep.

She had not sobbed this morning either, Albert remembered as he crossed the quiet Square. He had seen her lie with her eyes closed; she seemed to be staring at the inside of the lids. Standing in the room for some minutes, without evoking a response, Albert began to ask himself what would happen to the beautiful crystal and porcelain scent bottles if his mother should die. Then imagining that she was simply pretending to sleep he tiptoed away.

Albert had left the Square and was now walking up a side street. He wondered if his mother's eyes would still be closed when he arrived home. Grimaud would almost certainly be sitting in the darkness, ready to chastise.

As he recognized the awkward walk, then the harassed figure, of Dr. LeGrand emerging from the shadows Albert heard himself whisper:

'The silly old woman.'

Chapter 9

In the hours during which he waited for his son to return, Grimaud visited his wife's room on more than one occasion. As he paced past the sofa he sometimes found his steps taking him out of the study, and wondering why he was nervously climbing to her bedroom he reassured himself, as if in answer, with the thought that he need feel no remorse.

Standing at the end of the bed, glancing past her tray with its half-drunk, cold soup and untouched *biscotte*, he would ask:

'How are you feeling?' Grimaud's voice was low but gruff, almost strangled by his efforts to control it. 'Ivette. Can you hear me?' There was silence except for his heartbeats and the sound of her irregular breathing. After a pause, during which he passed a hand through his hair, he tried to coax her into conversation. 'Ivette. Why don't you speak to me?' If only he could draw a single word from her.

Even after Grimaud knew it was useless he continued talking. He could not accept that he had lost her. His voice became harsher, more abusive, until, unable to bear it any longer, he shouted out some insult. A second later he came clattering down the stairs.

Now, as he sat once more on his sofa, Grimaud's mind filled with memories. His mother's room had been dark although she had died in the mid-morning. His father, who rarely embraced her except when saying 'Goodbye' in public, leant over unsteadily and kissed a cheek with his eyes closed. For days after his face took on an abstracted expression whenever his mouth, its lips hanging slightly open, quivered.

Although Grimaud had already been married for several years by then his mother's death had left him feeling acutely vulnerable to his father. Despite the old man's virtual retirement from the business, Grimaud seemed to sense his continuing influence. It appeared to loom in a portrait; in his signature on out-of-date letters; in the cursive script with which he had insisted that all the clerks should write. Even more immediate than these palpable signs of his existence was the constant presence which Grimaud's father apparently maintained in his son's thoughts and cares. Grimaud needed to remind himself that his father was living with relations in Cairo. (Within eighteen months of his wife's funeral he too suddenly died.) Yet the old man's harsh voice, unsoftened by his wife's intervention or looks of pained silence, went on sounding in his son's ears as it had when Grimaud and his brother were boys.

Even more recently, while Grimaud was scrutinizing a file of documents or penning a letter, his mind went blank. He rubbed his eyes as the writing before him grew blurred. Then, tired and confused, he became aware of a testy inner voice disapproving of his recurrent inertia. It spoke in the hectoring tone which his father had used throughout Grimaud's youth:

'If only you *did* have the wisdom of Solomon!'

Yet disagreeable as his father had frequently been, Grimaud now told himself, sitting back in the sofa, one had to concede that his aims were largely correct. He could see just how admirable the old man's standards were, now that he was trying, though others made it difficult, to bring up a boy of his own. After all, application and probity could hardly be considered innate characteristics of children. Albert's deplorable behaviour had at least taught him that.

Grimaud recalled that when his father had bullied him into joining the business, then condemned his efforts without making concessions to his son's inexperience or age, his mother, though shocked, had resisted her child's attempts to draw her into conversations about his father. She raised her head high, with its imperious expression, and declared that they should be proud of him and all he had built. In time they would realize that his ideals, though few but he could attain to them, were truly worthwhile. Speaking for herself—she had pressed a clasped hand to the strands of her pearl necklace—she was sure that she would always be happy with a man whom she could honour and respect.

Grimaud often saw those fingers turn quite white as they grasped a necklace or locket. One evening when his father harangued him in the hall, saying that he would bring the firm to ruin with his inefficiency and indifference, she repeatedly adjusted her pendant cameo. And looking out from the drawing-room when her husband suddenly struck their son, her hand grew totally still: the fingers tightened.

Several hours later, when the old man had returned to the office and they were sitting alone, she kissed her son and asked how he was feeling. Then, suggesting that perhaps there was a grain of truth in what his father had said, her eyes seemed apologetic.

Grimaud remembered, when he began pacing once more in the study, how his mother's hands had alternatively fidgeted and trembled, at the end. The taut fingers, bulging at the knuckles and joints, no longer played with a brooch. They pulled at the sheet, at her nightdress, at their nails. Finally they had to be unlocked from each other.

Ivette now lay in that room. It became her's, Grimaud recalled, soon after her father-in-law had moved to Cairo. As Grimaud walked from the study and paused at the foot of the stairs, he seemed to see her dark, swollen hands. But clenching his fists and refusing to pay another fruitless visit to his wife, he reproved himself angrily for dwelling so much on his memories.

It was wrong to keep looking to the past. People who did so, like the Doctor, began to grow inert and pathetic. One could see how LeGrand's continual brooding on himself, doubtless the result of a solitary life, had rendered him anaemic and moody. He would rarely interrupt while a patient talked, but gazed with such a distant look on his face that one could not be sure if he was listening or dreaming. Then, uttering some conventionally sympathetic words, he ended by adding that things were rarely as bad as they seemed.

Grimaud only hoped that Albert, who had recently begun to strike him as strange, would not grow up to be equally soft or lifeless. He always tried to persuade the boy to model himself on great men. For unlike those idlers and thinkers who dwelt on the past, their eyes dead to the world around them, they judged and joined the progress of events. They added the strengths of their personalities to the movement of history.

It was largely Ivette's fault that Albert was so withdrawn and secretive. She had frequently pleaded with her husband not to be harsh with the boy; not to expect too much of a child; to remember that, as a baby, his health had been delicate. (But then, although even Napoleon had ordered the nursery to be padded when his young son had begun to walk, he had also thought tears unseemly in a future King of France.)

Of course, Ivette interfered with Grimaud's life as well. She suggested that he took the firm too seriously, or that he worked too hard and needed a holiday. She might sit on the arm of his chair and ruffle his carefully combed hair. He had even known her to play waltzes on the piano while he was reading. Their son, singing in the discordant treble voice which Grimaud had learnt to loathe, danced out of time to the music.

Of course, Grimaud thought as he remembered his wife lying silent and ill, he had formed little idea of Ivette's true character when they had first been married. It had only been much later that he could endorse the truth of his father's description of her as shallow and weak. She scarcely recognized Grimaud's vindication of himself in the firm, and now she cared nothing for the burnt cargo and charred ruins.

AN ARAB FUNERAL

In the early days Grimaud had loved Ivette so badly that it never occurred to him to try to see her personality whole. He longed for her less out of fondness for any positive features that she might possess than as a relief from the intolerable anxiety he felt when out of her presence. Even when they met, Grimaud was aware of little except himself. He was painfully conscious of his awkwardness in movement and speech; he feared that he would betray an odious compulsion to affront what was fragile and demure; he hated the bluff good-humour with which he tried to conceal his constant over-intensity.

Later, in the days when he could sit in the same room as Ivette without needing to hold her hand or kiss her, it seemed strange that her face had ever been inseparable from his thoughts. He concentrated on his letters, scarcely attending to her remarks; at the most he answered her questions curtly. It irritated him to see the fussy way in which she would arrange a bowl of flowers and then fold her arms, sighing as she stared out of the window. Freedom might have felt more precious to Ivette, he would think, if she were to do only a fraction of the work he did.

Grimaud resented her influence with their young son. He winced as he recalled the atmosphere of anxiousness and sentimentality that once pervaded the nursery. Each time Albert had fallen he had been examined for cuts, hugged, and given a sweet. Ivette simply never appreciated that it was vital for the heir to a business to be independent.

Nor did she realize how important the firm was to Grimaud. She made light of his industry, or sought to discourage it. When he had been decorated by the French Ambassador, Ivette herself coming from a family of distinguished lawyers, had taken her husband's achievement as a matter of course. She occupied herself more with ribbons and Albert's pranks than with acclaiming the extraordinary extent of Grimaud's efforts.

Although she arranged a dinner party for thirty guests as soon as the award had been announced, Grimaud knew that he could not take his wife's praise seriously. As she smiled at him knowingly across the candlelit table, gesturing with only the slightest inclination of her head while she graciously rebuffed playful compliments on her appearance, Grimaud was reminded of his father's habit of displaying a mock affection which only held good in public. Besides, even if Grimaud imagined Ivette's behaviour to be sincere, of what worth could it be since she was able to understand her husband so little? It had been a point of pride with Grimaud, ever since the earliest days in his father's firm, that he would never reveal the efforts which he had to make to achieve even minor goals, or his struggles to overcome a debilitating and irrational feeling of failure.

Sometimes Grimaud imagined that his wife had sensed his weakness, for all that, and spent her time laughing at it. She once made fun of him during the interval at a concert of piano music when he yawned and expressed a preference for military bands.

'But darling, that sort of thing's only for children.' Thereafter, each time she smiled, or merely creased the sides of her mouth, he felt that she thought him infantile, boorish, and inadequate.

If, as now, Grimaud occasionally sat alone, telling himself that after all there was nothing for her to know, he still could not rid his mind of the thought that, despite Ivette's shallowness, some basic fault, invisible to himself, lay naked to her eyes. Hearing giggling coming from the kitchen, he thought the joke was at his expense: he screwed up a memorandum, half-penned, and bawled out for silence. Or arriving home unexpectedly and finding his wife taking tea with some friends, he supposed that his seriousness had formed the hilarious subject for their conversation. Afterwards Ivette asked in vain why his greeting had been so peremptory.

Small things angered him most. When the back stud had broken, as he was hurriedly changing his wing collar in preparation for an evening engagement, he threw the pieces to the floor; and instead of calmly inserting a spare stud he marched into Ivette's dressing-room, violently rebuking her for committing him to a vacuous social life.

He denounced her more savagely still on the occasion on which he locked himself in the lavatory. Why it was that she should have chosen the moment when Grimaud was bellowing for someone to unscrew the door hinges to indulge her infuriating playfulness, by prolonging his incarceration, he did not understand. Long after he repeatedly rehearsed in his mind the pathetic sequence of events which had culminated in his slapping his near-hysterical wife.

As he continued to reflect he had felt an upsurge of guilt. His hands trembled to touch and smooth Ivette's reddened cheek: his own face seemed to be smarting. But his eyes flinched when they caught the gleam from her glance. He left the room with a fit of coughing.

Worst of all were the times when Grimaud suffered the reproaches implicit in his wife's long silences. One night, soon after Ivette's pregnancy had been diagnosed, he visited her bed only to have his advances rejected. Feeling that he had been treated with intolerable disdain, though aware that the Doctor had advised against intercourse even at this early stage, he sulkily observed her light hand resting on his arm.

'Don't!' he growled. 'You disgust me.'

For a while after Grimaud accepted that his behaviour had been offensive and unkind. Of course there had also been mitigating circumstances. He was tired, over-worked; and the discovery that she was pregnant had strained his wife, making her perfunctory and nervous. Nonetheless, Grimaud might have continued thinking that he had behaved in an extraordinary way had Ivette not met his hourly attempts to talk as if nothing had happened with silence. The rejection of a simulated normality—the only form of apology which Grimaud knew how to make—called forth impatience, then a return to his initial disgust and hatred.

In the succeeding weeks Grimaud observed his wife's dresses pinch at the waist: her entire stomach began bulging months later. He anticipated the way in which her visitors might recoil at the sight, and often secretly deplored nature's choice of such a disagreeable means of perpetuating the species. Finding it disconcerting for a process over which he had no control to be so obviously advancing apace, and suspecting the inroads which 'the happy event' would make into his patterned life and marriage, Grimaud wished that Ivette would advertise her condition less, by refraining from entertaining her friends and relatives. Yet much to his alarm she showed little enthusiasm at the prospect of effective purdah. Nor would she easily disband those female groups for whom the discussion of ailments was the focus of all animated society.

Ivette had been equally unco-operative, Grimaud now felt as he lay out full-length on the study sofa, during the months of her seemingly interminable illness. He had seen his vivacious young wife change through an almost ghostly process of degeneration into the silent, listless woman, who occupied a bedroom overhead. The smooth, white skin, on which he had once cooled his lips, gave way to tired flesh from which his hand withdrew as if by instinct. Her eyes, originally tender, spiteful, and agitated in turn, were glazed and deadened by sickness.

Why was it then, he wondered, that his wife resisted the Doctor's attempts to diagnose her malady? For whereas Grimaud overcame his own feeling of revulsion at LeGrand's insistence on pulling the Chinese screen about Ivette's swollen legs, in accordance with the latest French medical practices, she protested with shouts which had been both unnecessary and embarrassing. Immediately after the Doctor withdrew his scarred face from scrutinizing the body, raw with bedsores, and folded back the screen, her expression was of untold relief: she sank back again, as if insensible, onto the pillows. And watching the scene, Grimaud was troubled by the sudden certainty that his wife neither wished, nor was able, to recover.

On the subsequent occasions when he sensed this brute fact he felt faint, sick, and remote from his surroundings. In the office the clerks, copying their columns of figures, seemed to agitate their right arms from the elbows down, for no reason. While at meals, facing his son, Grimaud would let the cutlery drop from his hands and get up to escape the deafening drone of mosquitoes.

Soon the recognition of his wife's real state no longer dawned and set in Grimaud's mind. The ineluctable truth settled permanently. This awareness, as unsought as its accompaniment of continuous gloom, flared up into fits of uncontrollable panic.

How could she leave him? What had he done wrong? Had he failed, that she wished to end their life together? And with a voice so choked that it had sounded like anger, as he stood by her bed, he rebuked her for her very weakness. If she loved him, valued the things he had done for her sake, she would surely make this last effort!

During the hours which Grimaud had just spent in his study, after the last outburst, he had cursed the literalism with which his mind invariably viewed things. It would have been better he felt, as he began pacing about the room, to be a frivolous man who ignored unpleasant facts and enjoyed a self-deluded existence. Grimaud longed to exchange his temperament, personality, character even—though it had been so hard won—for those of a superficial Greek millionaire, whose invitations to dinner he had never accepted. Yet despite his regrets, and the ingenuity with which he imagined life to be other than it was, Grimaud could not blot out from his mind the true situation.

Eventually, thinking of Ivette's body invaded by disease and of that part of the business which had been ravaged by Arab rioters, he became convinced that a similar malignancy was at work in his room. It seemed to charge the atmosphere in his study. Monsters, whose phantom presence he had long sensed, materialized out of the shadows. Claws, beaks, and even wings stood out from chairs. He held still, trembling with terror. Telling himself that he should be courageous, but knowing that he was weak, he ran out of the room shouting for Albert. As his son came towards him, out of the night, Grimaud continued his ranting.

PART III
Almost a Year Later

A Jewish Funeral

Chapter 10

Suddenly the music soared. Angels embroidered in gold thread appeared to hover in the rich, dense sound. Perhaps their forms might leave the silken drapes and join the shadows cast by candlelight. At the very top, where the curtains almost touched the ceiling, Daniel Benchimol imagined that a group of cherubim had floated free, liberated by the long crescendo. Yet as he watched, a gentle breeze tilted whole flocks of the little creatures away from him. Some almost disappeared around a fold. Only their calves and tiny feet suggested that they would sway back in a moment.

Daniel saw the disturbance pass beyond the heavy fabric. It drew on fragile flames, causing a lady's curls to quiver. Then catching up strands of hair from glistening heads in the orchestra, in the imposing presence of a David portrait of Napoleon, the current seemed to lose its force.

Daniel knew that this shudder would usually have passed unnoticed by the audience in the Hotel San Stefano. For that matter, so might an uncertain performance of the *Eroica* symphony. Gentlemen dressed for dinner, lounging against the foyer pillars which marked the perimeter of the concert hall, generally made more noise by whispering than they would have done by talking aloud. Their wives only added to the unscored hum by turning back in their seats to ask for silence. Yet since the riot, over nine months past, Daniel had often noticed how groups of Europeans could be unnerved by the most commonplace interruptions. A creaking door, a barking dog, the sounds of Arabic coming through a wall, or even the gradual darkening of a room as afternoon gave way to evening, reduced a conversation to frozen silence. And now, as Daniel glanced at the other members of his party, he noticed LeGrand staring apprehensively at the fluttering curtains, while M. Grimaud, seated next to his nine-year-old son, looked through the window as if into the eyes of a murderer.

Daniel had sensed the tension during dinner, an hour before the concert. Their host, the Doctor, constantly looked round at the waiters. Then, having stirred his coffee for longer than necessary, he looked at the cup, raised it to his lips, and added with a weak smile:

'I wonder if it's poisoned.'

Benchimol had recently heard LeGrand make the same remark whenever he held a teacup between his fat thumb and forefinger at the Hotel Cecil. Daniel found his predictability irritating. More annoying still was the dullness, the lack of spirit, which underlay the Doctor's repetitiveness. It rendered him nervous and weak in this time of crisis.

Daniel remembered how different it had all been in his student days. They queued all morning, and sometimes all night, for concert and opera tickets. One would never have suspected that Paris had been under siege. Exuberant audiences clapped between movements and demanded an encore at the end of each aria. (As he reminisced, Daniel sometimes found himself wishing that his life could be as exciting again.) People cried with emotion as they sang the *Marseillaise* in public places. Even hearing the thud of artillery coming from behind the Prussian lines, some continued enjoying kangaroo soup in restaurants as they drank up the special reserves of *Romanée-Conti* and *Château d'Yquem*.

Daniel recalled crowds gathering around balloons in the parks. People came to watch messengers carrying dispatches take off for the French army outside Paris. Everyone gasped as the excess gas was ignited. Then all heads followed the blue and gold spheres as they rose, pulling up their loaded baskets from the lawns. Drifting through clouds into the sunlit sky, the balloons passed over lakes, palaces, and fountains. Soaring across woods and fields, they had finally crossed the enemy encampments.

Now, over seven years later, it was as if Benchimol could hear the boom of cannon again in the triumphal music. Parisian cheers seemed to swell from the trembling earth, while each balloon floated on, out of the range of gunfire. Even LeGrand was stirred by the sounds. He tapped his fingers to notes played almost in time, on the back of an inanimate hand. And the Emperor, whose victories this symphony had once been intended to celebrate, appeared to command the entire concert hall from a copy of his portrait hanging over the orchestra.

Lately Daniel had noticed a version of *Napoleon in His Study* on some wall in most French houses. He often looked at the sword, the general's epaulettes, and the medal of the Legion of Honour—marks of Bonaparte's authority—while tutoring boys or drinking aperitifs with their parents. Italians, Greeks, and Jews, doubtless similarly prompted by recent events to relish the memory of European military successes in Egypt, also prominently displayed the Emperor in their rooms. Yet Daniel doubted if such reverence was altogether well-directed. There was surely something theatrical in an image of Napoleon posing for the painter only after a long night's work in the service of his people. The all-too-obvious symbolism of a clock reading 4.13, and low burning candles, indicated a meretricious nature. Again, Napoleon's was hardly an untarnished success story; nor was he especially renowned for his exemplary end. But then people who idolized historical figures were prepared to make heroes of the most unsuitable persons in their attempts to turn away from a seemingly intolerable present.

Daniel had long known that it was idle to pine for the

past. After all, his own breach with his childhood and youth was now total. In deserting the family and its business for a precarious future as a writer he had shown a disdain for his parents' values, which they would hardly forgive. So if he sometimes tired of the scrappy life to which teaching, his sole means of support, had reduced him, he forbade himself wistful backward glances at the luxury he had once enjoyed in his home. Besides, memory invariably distorted what had actually happened: reminiscences grew out of those moods of nostalgia and sentimentality with which most people tried to escape the unpleasant realities of life.

Daniel felt that a less superficial view of history showed that no golden ages had ever existed. All epochs were as grey as the present. There were no Elysian fields. He had seen, even in his own twenty-nine short years, how an unromantic period like the first siege of Paris had been falsely represented in countless memoirs and conversations as heroic and idealistic.

At that time every Parisian had prayed for wind, but soon hope, and then courage, faltered. Balloons, carrying urgent return messages from Gambetta's armies in the provinces, hovered in the distance like tantalizing baits. They were prevented from riding back to the capital by the prevailing westerly air currents. So everyone was forced to wait for relief until well into the winter. By then there were blizzards and ice over the Seine.

Daniel, like most others, begrudged being conscripted. It was so cold that they used almost all the army furniture as fuel. Later, escaping from the barrack in the small hours of the morning, they felled prize trees in a nearby botanical garden. Soldiers without boots hobbled down snowy roads with sackcloth for footwear. Everyone was suffering from frostbite and scurvy. Once a horse-drawn hearse pulled up for a moment before a group of National Guardsmen. By the time the driver and his assistant returned the Guards had disappeared: the coffin and harness were empty.

January saw the worst. At times, during the twenty-three nights of Prussian bombardment, they were reduced to eating coagulated horses' blood. The din of artillery seemed to persist even after Daniel left his billet, a freezing cellar, and walked into the silent street. He saw strips of bright paper hanging limply from the inside walls of shattered houses. Ornamental plaster, saturated with melting snow, flaked away from the exposed ceilings of restaurants. Mirrors, pomanders, candelabra, and all the personal items in bedrooms, were dulled, then obscured by layers of sleet. Only the whine of a mongrel, echoing through ruined passageways, had reminded him that no battle gave rise to the reverberations which still filled his head.

The orchestra, loud if not urgent with victory, roused Daniel from his reminiscences. Once more the angelic hosts seemed to soar. Bonaparte looked on, clean shaven and, for the moment, Imperial. Grimaud returned the stern gaze, fondling his untrimmed black beard. These uncultivated strands summoned up a further face from Daniel's mind. It hovered there, unheeded, with the same goatee and glistening eyes as Grimaud's. Only gradually did Daniel realize that during the last few seconds he had been thinking of Napoleon III.

Of course, if a monarch like Louis Napoleon had been captivated by the cult of the first Napoleon it was unlikely that a mere millionaire would escape its power. Daniel watched Albert's father explore the portrait intently. Grimaud was touching his own lips so gently that they might have been relics of the Emperor's mouth. Whatever thoughts occupied Grimaud's mind at this moment, Daniel felt sure that they were not the kind of uncomplimentary reflections on Napoleon I's career which, had they been known to Napoleon III, might have curtailed Imperial designs culminating in the defeat at Sedan and, indirectly, the first siege of Paris. Grimaud's forcible expression of his views at dinner had made it plain that he was not a man to dwell on defeats: his hero had surely never retreated from Russia, lost a battle at Waterloo, or died on St. Helena. Nor was he probably sensitive to the reason why Beethoven had torn up his dedication of this symphony: Napoleon's hubris in crowning himself Emperor.

It had been LeGrand who had introduced education as the topic of discussion. (They were dipping *cornichons* and lettuce hearts into the salt as they paused between courses.) Yet Daniel imagined that the Doctor hoped to find a subject of mutual interest to a father and a schoolmaster meeting for the first time, rather than the starting-point for Grimaud's shrill speech about life. On the previous occasions when Daniel had been invited to dinner a trite remark made by LeGrand early on in the meal had successfully encouraged polite exchanges between the guests for the rest of the evening.

Daniel was well aware that in general the Doctor nursed little interest in novels, syllabuses, or history. His comments over tea at the Cecil usually touched on little except the contents of the cake trolley. But, having apparently taken a liking to young Benchimol, LeGrand had decided to introduce him to his distinguished acquaintances—for the most part no strangers to illness. They might help Daniel establish himself as a writer once they heard his views on literature and art.

Daniel winced and rubbed his broad forehead as the Doctor diverted the course of each conversation to refer to the vulgarity of new French poets, or the strange colours used by modern painters: his cue had been hard to overlook. And caring scarcely more for the way he himself, an unmistakable protégé, duly elaborated on these themes, than for the lack of conviction with which LeGrand made essays in the sphere of culture, Daniel dismissed his association with the Doctor. After all, it was hardly a sign of close friendship to accept an occasional dinner invitation from somebody with whom one could only be intimate on the subject of one's liver. While tea taken together, *faute de mieux*, at the somnolent hour in a foreign city, could only look like companionship to eyes sadder than Benchimol's.

Sitting in the restaurant before the concert, Daniel had

found himself wondering why he passed so much time in the company of someone to whom he was indifferent. It was not out of self-interest, he was sure. M. Grimaud, a businessman, presumably lacked the influence to advance Daniel's writings; besides, he made clear his intolerance of art.

'Poetry, novels—perhaps they're all right for dreamers and idlers. But what use are they for people who want to *do* things in this life? Besides, literature is a bad influence on children. Eventually they'll have to take their place in a real world. And just look at the kind of rubbish that's written these days.' He glowered at Benchimol, who had previously expressed a desire to give up teaching as soon as he had published some poems and short stories. 'It's completely depraved; no one even mentions the great virtues like ambition or courage any more.'

Daniel had certainly been led to expect that Grimaud's behaviour might appear somewhat strange. The Doctor had warned him that although his patient had now largely recovered from the riots, both financially and emotionally, he was still under strain. No matter how relaxed and rested he sometimes seemed, Grimaud was subject to recurrent nervous collapses which his wife's illness, or the troubled times, could catalyze without warning. For all that, Daniel did not expect to be addressed with such scant regard for the civilities of normal society. His aims and ambitions were dismissed with the brutality which an Arab might display towards his child.

Daniel told himself that Grimaud did not so much offend his pride as his sense of good taste. Despite the man's fine clothes and knowledge of wines, his attitudes were transparently vulgar. When Grimaud used examples from the past to show that human progress demanded the agency of great men, his arguments were as shrill, opinionated, and ill-informed as Napoleon's discourses on history. After all, what evidence was there for the progress of mankind? Most people's lot had never been improved. One simply needed to look at the Arabs to realize that. Only blind stupidity could support Grimaud's materialist creed when it was obvious that there neither had been, nor would be, a paradise on earth.

Doubtless Grimaud imagined that he was the hero of his age. With his financial Empire and unique insight into the real object of Arab hatred—the Jews, not the Europeans—he was the veritable engine of history. And Albert was obviously destined to continue his life's work. (The boy had contradicted his father throughout the meal; preferring capon to fish, refusing to try the wine, disputing the hours at which it was safest to walk in the street.) Yet Daniel wondered why Grimaud could not see that each generation must fail to advance the achievements of the preceding one. Man's flaws, not his successes, were passed on from father to son: they inhibited human development.

It was not the first time that Daniel had considered these things. Similar thoughts had occurred to him far from the concerts at San Stefano. In a Paris cellar, listening to the advancing Prussian guns, he had seen Napoleon III's image obscured by slime. Soldiers sat gambling away the hours, throwing their near-worthless Imperial coins to the ground. Daniel grew to loathe the exaggerated moustache which Thiers had once advised his monarch to shave; he hated those passionate eyes. Even so, Daniel might have simply dismissed the man's preposterous attempts to further Napoleon I's designs and style had they not reduced him to a subterranean cave where he had suffered with rheumatism, hunger, and chilblains.

Unlike most of his contemporaries, Daniel did not participate in the political movements of the next few years. It was not, he now felt, apathy on his part. After all, few could have remained indifferent to the momentous events overtaking the capital: the second siege, the rise and fall of the Commune. Rather, he had once seen great hopes dashed, and thereafter mistrusted even noble political ambitions. In sailing to Alexandria as a poet, Daniel set his face against Paris and his country's destiny. He had turned from the fortunes of his father's business and the world of public affairs.

Today, some time before the concert, Daniel had been looking at great men in the Greco-Roman Museum. Statues stared across the deserted halls with wide, marble eyes. Busts of kings and friezes of emperors riding in triumph, appeared blanched and remote in the mid-afternoon sun. Only an occasional figure betrayed the provenance of its heroism. There were hints in the arresting tilt of a head or pursing of lips, gestures with which sculptors had momentarily, as it must once have seemed, defied the convention of majestic impersonality demanded by their craft. Yet Daniel doubted whether mere clues could provide the substance for a poem. He had envisaged a satirical ode to heroes that would leave urns and Olympus untouched.

Now, hours later, as most of the orchestra drew towards its ultimate crescendo, Daniel found himself re-examining Napoleon I's face. It was impassive and inscrutable, like the classical heads in the Museum. Bonaparte, no less than such Emperors, was an anthropoid God. As he looked away Daniel noticed M. Grimaud attending to the symphony's victorious finale with heavy eyes and a trembling beard. The embroidered angels were soaring about his head. Then Daniel knew that his best way lay through private histories. Personal lives, not public faces, would reveal the strange dramas and hard ironies which had helped mould heroic wills.

Chapter 11

As the Doctor entered a narrow passage his hand trailed over the surface of mud walls. It touched the door hinges on Arab houses. He once felt crumbling brick. Only when his fingers drew back from coarse, rodent-like hairs did he realize that he was lost: a cord, clotted with plaster, was projecting from a half-finished room.

Until now LeGrand had been returning from the concert almost by instinct. He walked carelessly down moon-lit avenues, and ambled through public gardens and squares. All the time he hummed themes from the symphony. And occasionally, staring up at the night sky, he felt that San Stefano was a vivid dream.

He remembered that as they had entered the hotel, hall porters had been training the wicks on oil lamps. Waiters carried candelabra through the restaurant, lit by chandeliers. Crystal glasses split the light into reds, blues, and violets: they magnified the threads of bubbles rising from champagne. And in the foyer, where they later heard the music, emeralds and diamonds had gleamed and glittered . . .

Suddenly, entering the dark alley, LeGrand found that the image had faded. San Stefano, with its wide, marble floor and sea breezes, was like an ephemeral vision, an unreal memory belonging to somebody else.

Still, it had been a good evening. The Doctor tried to reassure himself with the thought as he felt a shudder of panic at finding himself lost at such an hour in this dangerous quarter. Perhaps if he were to continue along the passage he would emerge near his flat. Then he might sit smoking in his rocking-chair, gazing into the darkness. He would sway, watched by the maid, for some time before going to bed.

On each occasion that LeGrand had recently forsaken his evening routine—the surgery was usually followed by an aperitif, supper, and a solitary pipe—he found it hard to regain his emotional balance. He could not rest until he had pieced together the conversation at dinner. Only after he recalled every nuance, pondering over opaque phrases and wincing at caustic remarks, would he consider retiring. He continued rehearsing the arguments long after yawning; he might stare into space as he stood scratching his head.

The Doctor even feared for his peace of mind, so painstakingly established, while preparing to meet his guests. His lips would mouth the words with which he intended to introduce M. Benchimol, as he surveyed his thinning hair

71

in the mirror. And hoping that Daniel would prove more lively, less aggressive, than usual, he felt pangs of despair at squandering a gift of English lavender water on his discoloured cheek.

Tonight, at least, had proved a good evening. He still thought so as he gingerly made his way down the dark alley. At first LeGrand had been anxious lest his choice of guests should prove unsuccessful. For in providing opportunities for people to make each others' acquaintance —he was never really sure if anyone cared to make his— he always risked introducing persons who would dislike one another. And while he had known some antipathies to express themselves in witty verbal exchanges and epigrammatic repartees, he doubted whether Grimaud and Benchimol would confine their remarks to the boundaries of humour once their tempers were aroused.

Of course, the Doctor had thought as they entered the restaurant, he had less to fear from Solomon Grimaud. It was true that LeGrand had heard him raise his voice in anger more than once. But that was when the poor man was at his most wretched, in the days when his warehouses and cargoes were destroyed. Grimaud had now made good the injuries to his business, or at least so one gathered. (LeGrand was vague as to exactly how.) Besides, his bearing witnessed a former dignity. If he continued to lead a tranquil life he might even regain his old presence and poise.

Benchimol, by contrast, had recently seemed more and more tense. Although the Doctor enjoyed his company, perhaps even feeling responsible for him in a way that he had not felt for anybody since his nephew had left for France, he sometimes found it hard to overlook the young man's manner. Daniel had no excuse for his misanthropic behaviour. He had few commitments in his life; no business to be carried on under precarious conditions; no invalid wife.

LeGrand was now emerging from the suffocating passage. In a few further steps he left the Arab quarter. And unexpectedly recognizing the houses and streets, he again found himself singing the tunes of triumph.

'Don't you think you're a little lavish with your praise?'
he remembered Daniel asking when he had approved of the
orchestra's performance after the concert. They were
standing on the hotel steps, talking as they watched the
Grimauds' carriage pull away. 'The orchestra sounded as
if it was running a race. And personally I find that Beethoven can seem almost strident.' How affected Benchimol
could sometimes be! The Doctor grew angry, recalling his
dry, captious voice. There had surely been no reason for
Daniel to be so querulous, so lacking in *joie de vivre*. The
more LeGrand tried to help his young friend recently, the
less gratitude he received in return. It was almost as if
Daniel disliked the Doctor for his kindness, his dinner
parties and introductions. What other explanation could
there be for such hurtful remarks? They had made
LeGrand feel almost despicable for enjoying strong, all-
embracing music.

At least M. Grimaud had not yielded passively to
Daniel's opinions. He had been forceful, loud even, in
proclaiming his own. After claiming that the aim of 'true'
education was the formation of character, and that music
and literature were inadequate to this task, Grimaud was
interrupted by Daniel:

'But it takes a much stronger character to become a
writer than you seem to think. After all, does one need
more will-power to give up a comfortable life in order to
pursue an artistic career, or to sit behind a secure business
desk?'

'I don't dispute that it takes great strength of will to do
what you're doing,' Grimaud answered with an air of
politeness. 'But in fairness I should add that will-power is
required to knock one's head against a brick wall. Yet
nobody suggests that brick walls should become a
principle of education.'

'M. Grimaud,' Daniel replied in a voice made almost
pompous by restrained irritation, 'education is my
profession . . .'

'Young man, I could not be more impressed if you were
to tell me that your's was the oldest profession in the

world.' And allowing time for his sour smile to fade, Grimaud continued: 'I have had my son educated privately out of profound mistrust for members of your profession. I never want him to have to go to a school.'

'Why can't I go to school?'

LeGrand remembered how the nine-year-old voice, moody from the persistent company of adults, had seemed to emerge from another conversation to which nobody but Albert was privy.

'Because I say so.' The child had sighed at his father's answer. 'I'm afraid, young man, that you already have too much of your own way.'

Approaching the flat, the Doctor noticed his maid leaning over the veranda in darkness. Once inside, he did not trouble her to light a lamp. She stared while he threw his jacket on the back of the rocking-chair. It hung as though from cadaverous shoulders. LeGrand sat smoking, swaying before the gauze curtains.

'I've had a good evening.' The maid could not tell if the whispered remark was intended for her.

Chapter 12

As the carriage pulled away from San Stefano Albert's father grew silent. He leaned back in the leather seat and stroked the wisps of his beard, noticing LeGrand and Benchimol still chatting on the hotel steps. Then focusing his eyes over the cabby's shoulder, he stared into the distance. It was still, except for shreds of cloud occasionally crossing the stars.

Albert sat quietly too. He had no desire to re-awaken his father's anger. It seemed that even innocent words, like those he had spoken at dinner, could provoke M. Grimaud's fury. It was best to be silent and look straight before him. Yet although the boy's head only moved with the rhythmical jolt of the horse and the slight lurch of the cab as it abruptly turned corners, he could still see his father's stern face from the corner of an eye. Once, when the driver suddenly pulled up before a landau slowly drawing into the corniche from a side street, Albert was thrown towards his father. He looked up, but M. Grimaud chose to disregard the warm weight momentarily burdening his shoulder: his shadowy features had settled into a scowl.

They trundled along the straight coastline. It was dark except for the occasional glow of charcoal braziers on which Arab vendors toasted their maize beneath palms. Sometimes Albert noticed a light in the distance. He could not tell if it came from the city. Perhaps it was a low star, or a ship anchored in the harbour. Fixing his eyes on what he eventually decided was a shifting lantern, Albert pretended that the void surrounding the carriage was sea. Tonight he lay alone in a boat lapped by gentle waves. Their motions were regular; they sounded like horses' hooves . . . Soon there was the crack of a whip. The Arab driver gave a dry cough and spat as they halted before the metal gates. Albert's father was reaching vigorously into his pockets for change.

Mme Grimaud heard her husband and son walk up the gravel path.

'Albert,' she called out as they entered the house. Just as the boy began crossing the hall to go up to his mother's bedroom, Grimaud shouted:

'Don't!' He almost flinched before Albert's searching eyes. Then turning away sharply, he added in a gruff voice: 'Leave her. She shouldn't be disturbed.'

Albert did not undress for some time. He sat on the edge of his bed, staring into the light entering the half-open door.

'Albert darling!' He paused uncertainly before getting up. Then seeing his father pace from the study to the foot of the stairs he fell back on the bed. He watched Grimaud return to his study.

Albert could hear his father walking about long after he had blown out his candle. He wondered if he might enter his room: he almost expected him to push the door open.

Suddenly the boy jerked forward, not sure if he was still dreaming, certain that somebody was standing by the bed. It was not the first time he had sensed another presence. On previous occasions he had continued to see figures in the shapes of chairs and draperies long after he had realized that he was alone. Now again he felt too frightened to move, although he could hear the breathing, reassuring and regular, coming from his parents' rooms.

As he looked back at his sleepless night, the next afternoon, he felt that he had wriggled and tossed days, even years ago. At present he was mounting one of his father's horses at the Sporting Club. The sun elongated the bluish grass, fusing the tip of each blade with its brilliant light. He looked down, unseeingly, at the track. When he recalled the events which had occurred a mere few hours before, the cool house with its tall, shady trees seemed improbable and unreal.

Albert remembered sitting with his mother that morning when his tutor had left. Grimaud returned for lunch soon after.

'I'm back!' he called, slamming the front door behind him. Neither answered. 'Where are you both?' he demanded, applying a handkerchief to the back of his neck. Then crossing the hall, he intercepted Albert, ambling downstairs from his mother's bedroom. 'What've you been doing up there?'

The boy did not answer any more than he had replied to Grimaud's first two remarks. He did not know what to say. He simply walked into the dining-room where a maid was moving a vase of pink zinnias from the table which she was laying for lunch.

'Where do you think you're going? Come here when I'm talking to you.' Albert sighed and made his way back to the hall. He noticed the sweat glistening on his father's beard; beads were hanging from his eyebrows. 'Now what were you talking about with your mother? Tell me. I want to know.'

'Nothing,' Albert answered sullenly, looking vaguely into the distance.

'Don't lie! You were talking about me behind my back.'

'No we weren't!' Albert protested as his father took him by the forearm.

'Now listen to me. It's about time certain things were made clear.' Albert pulled himself away. He started moving back to the foot of the stairs. 'I don't want you to keep going into your mother's bedroom.'

'Why not?'

'Because I don't.'

'But she calls me.'

'Don't argue! If I say you mustn't—' he cuffed the back of Albert's head—'you mustn't. And if I catch you up there again I'll beat you to within an inch of your life!' He shouted it out as Albert rushed up the stairs and threw himself onto his mother's counterpane.

'I *will* see her if I want to,' the boy shrieked hysterically. Grimaud followed him, and raising a hand to pull him from the bed, bawled at his bewildered wife:

'You just lie there encouraging him!'

'Don't hit my mother!' Albert drew his hand from the swollen fingers in which she enclosed it. Clenching his fists, he beat against his father's chest. Grimaud shook him away and tried, unsuccessfully, to grip Albert's wrists.

'Stop it! Stop it both of you!' Mme Grimaud's lips trembled as she whispered. She sank back onto the pillows. Her breathing continued wheezing and erratic.

Albert was the first to leave the room. His right eye twitched when he turned away from his father. But then, he remembered as the horse took its first paces at the Sporting Club hours later, he had been served lunch at the head of the polished table. His father, claiming that he was no longer hungry, had trudged into the study.

'You know you're not supposed to ride this horse,' the wrinkled Arab groom said, looking up at Albert. He was patting the courser's chestnut haunches with his soft, brown hand. 'Why can't you take your own pony? Your father would be furious if he ever found out that you'd been riding his horse.'

Albert did not really know why he suddenly wanted to

mount such a powerful animal. All he could say was that leaving the noiseless house, just after lunch, he had run over the lawn; and that racing through the sunshine he felt airy and light. It seemed that he could fly like the blue butterflies hovering over the surface of cypresses. Watching them quiver and soar, he had known that there was nothing over which he could not rise.

Urging on the horse, rising and falling in the saddle, Albert did not recall running through the streets to the Sporting Club. He was only aware of the breeze freshening his cheeks as he rode faster. Trying to tighten his knees, the green track merged into the stables and sea.

'You must never go near my horses,' his father seemed to be saying. Albert pictured him strutting about in his white breeches and brown boots, carrying an ivory-handled crop. The face vibrated for a few seconds; it grew blurred in the mid-afternoon heat.

The groom watched Albert pass him. He was pleased to see his back so erect. He had often straightened the boy's shoulders and impressed on him the importance of rhythm and style. The rider, all in white, called out to the stallion in a voice as yet unbroken. The groom saw him lean right forward and rest his head against the animal's neck. Lurching with the galloping horse, Albert dug both heels into its glistening ribs.

Nothing could stop him now. He was Pegasus. He was climbing the sky round this bend. Far away, blue, green, and sand mixed behind him. At each side, there would flash clusters of stars. Now at last he was entering areas where his actions would never be controlled . . . Yet once more there whirled harsh images; angry voices, faces with beards. But soon the hooves had pounded and passed them. The ferocious features undid in the wind.

The groom saw the horse returning. It was moving parallel to a low fence. As its great hooves flicked between the rails, he felt a mixture of admiration and concern for the rider. Observing that Albert had started to sway he tried to give him advice. But the horse was galloping faster. The boy was slouched uneasily in the saddle.

The track was now eclipsed behind Albert. Coloured space spilled out at each side. Only intense light lay before him. He was rising into the sun. He turned away, blinking. The earth lurched and advanced. The more he tried to sit up in the saddle, the more slippery the reins seemed.

The groom jumped over the fence, shouting to him to slow down. But Albert did not hear him as the horse bolted. There was now only the noise of hooves and a painful pulsing in his head. Then there was a moment of darkness. The sun tilted and turned.

The groom backed away from the stallion. The animal had raised its front legs and head. With a terrible snorting it appeared to perform a grotesque dance. And rearing even higher, it discharged the boy.

Albert saw the sun falling. He did not remember joining it through the still afternoon air. By then he had entered regions containing strange creatures: winged horses, winged heels, and a winged youth tumbling through the sea.

Chapter 13

At first there was a filament of light. It reached out of the darkness. Then there were luminous waves. They almost flooded Albert's eyes as they surged from his bedside oil lamp. He sat up.

'Just lie still. Don't try to move.' The Doctor was looking at him from the arm-chair. It was evening.

Albert squinted and turned, noticing his bandaged left leg as if it did not belong to him. He found that he could not stir the toes. They were numb. Nor was there any sensation in the rest of the splinted limb.

'It's a miracle that you weren't badly hurt. As it is, I think that you'll live. You should be back on your feet in a couple of weeks. You must've been mad, a little fellow like you riding that enormous horse.'

LeGrand had continued speaking in his low, monoton-
ous voice. It droned on, somehow merging into the
shadows. By then the boy was no longer listening. He felt
so faint that he seemed to be floating.

For days after, Albert's mind seemed to wander through
cycles of day dreaming, reverie, and sleep. He was roused
for various medicines at different intervals. He was given
boiled food and warm milk, despite the heat. Once M.
Benchimol visited him. The boy did not know why. He sat
on the edge of the bed, talking while Albert was docile,
listening when he grew manic.

'I should be back on my feet in a couple of weeks. Then
I'll have my own stallion.'

'Well, I doubt whether that's such a good idea.'
Benchimol put a hand on Albert's bruised forehead. 'You
still have rather a fever.'

As he went, M. Benchimol left a present. Albert opened
it carefully. (He could re-use the wrapping paper and
string.) It was a book containing illustrations. But why
were the words *Lycée Français—Alexandrie* stamped in
purple ink on the pages? The phrase was repeated on a
picture of a Greek prince. Albert noticed from the caption
that his name derived from his limp. The boy had soon
read all the accounts of Hellenic myths. It seemed that
everyone was related and had died violently.

Somewhat later Albert was occasionally allowed out of
bed. He moved about with the help of one of his father's
sticks. Hobbling through the house in the mid-morning, he
could hear the servants' voices. They would be laughing
and chattering with the toothless Arab woman who
delivered lemons to the kitchen. Albert might be considering that this felt like a holiday, his lessons having
recently been suspended, when the Doctor would say:

'Now let's go and see your mother.'

It would be dark as Albert entered her room. Standing
at the foot of her bed, he could not tell if she was sleeping
or staring into the pillow. The blind was pulled at least
halfway down; hair brushes, mirrors, coloured bottles and
pairs of shoes, had all lost their outlines.

A JEWISH FUNERAL

Mme Grimaud turned her head towards the Doctor as he sat on the chair beside her. Glimpsing her son, she tried to raise herself on the pillows.

'Now don't get agitated,' LeGrand said. 'You must save your strength.'

Albert felt that there had always been the smell of medicine in the room. Recently he had also noticed the sweet odour of old bedclothes. Once when his mother was holding his hand, Albert saw that the front buttons of her nightdress were undone. They revealed limp breasts. She held him tighter as he had tried to move away.

'You'd better go back to your room,' the Doctor eventually whispered, easing Albert's mother back onto her pillows. But the boy was beginning to find his confinement as an invalid suffocating. He preferred fresh air and sunlight. He hobbled across the lawn in a dressing-gown. Resting in a wickerwork chair, he extended the clumsy leg. Its thousand nerves were tingling and live. Staring remotely at his bluish toes, he regretted that he found it so awkward to move. Of course, the Doctor had said that he would soon be well. But how could he wait to run into the sea curving away at his feet?

One morning LeGrand went straight up to Mme Grimaud's room without bothering to see Albert. Recently he had been examining the boy less and less. He would merely ask him how he felt and satisfy himself with general answers. Yet entering Mme Grimaud's door, he saw her son standing next to her. Albert was watching his mother sleeping, with an intense expression.

As usual the Doctor held her wrist, though he hardly attended to her pulse. He was looking at the boy's eyes. There was the steady purr of the oil lamp. It softened Mme Grimaud's face, giving a luminous glow to her features. There was even a suggestion of brown in her hair.

Discarding the wrist, LeGrand whispered:

'She's sleeping.' And leading Albert onto the landing he added: 'We must all make life peaceful for her now. I'm afraid she may . . .' he extended the soft palm of his hand '. . . she may be ill for some time.' LeGrand drew his fingers back. He looked down at the ground, suddenly moody.

Thereafter Albert's mother hardly ate. She left the toast that the maid served with her chicken soup, and soon she did not eat solid food at all. She would lie in bed, unable to hoist herself into a sitting position to be spoon-fed. When Albert or the Doctor visited her, she barely recognized them.

'Gilbert!' she would call, or 'Adolphe!', names whose significance could only be suspected.

As time passed she could no longer even drink her soup. It would fall from her mouth and dribble, unchecked, down her chin and nightdress. Or retaining a spoonful in her mouth, her chest and shoulders would convulse until she vomited it out. Eventually she lost all control over her bowels. When she defecated she whimpered until the maids, harassed by the constant demands which the illness made upon them, washed her, changed her, and opened the windows.

When Albert entered the room, his leg now out of splints, he might find her singing songs learnt in the nursery, with a gurgling sound. And if he caught her attention, her brow would knit and tears would stand in her eyes.

Towards the end she was always silent. She lay with her eyes closed, unmoving and unconscious. Albert could not believe that the mother he remembered was the same person as this invalid.

At five o'clock one afternoon LeGrand visited her as usual. He entered, wiping the sweat from his face. The maid who closed the door was on the verge of tears.

'Sh!' he said.

As the Doctor took Mme Grimaud's pulse he noticed that she was struggling for breath. From time to time she would emit a cry which sent tremors through her body. He gave her a sedative but she still continued to fight. At last the Doctor told the maid to call Albert's father.

'Tell him there isn't much time.'

Albert watched the agony with which his mother drew

in every breath. He clawed into the side of the arm-chair, afraid that each might be the last. When she called his name he ran to her side and would have fallen on her neck had LeGrand not guided him away.

'Would you rather wait outside?' the Doctor said. But though Albert had to hold his hand to his mouth in order to choke back his tears, he shook his head and remained.

After five minutes she could hardly breathe at all. She raised her head and with an effort, which Albert thought superhuman, opened her eyes. She looked terrified as she gulped in the air. Whining, her eyes still open, she sank back into the pillow. Suddenly she was still.

Albert did not move. The Doctor leaned over and lightly hooded her eyes with their lids. Albert, now fully realizing what had happened, tried to embrace his mother. The Doctor intercepted him and led him away from the room in which she lay.

Outside the sun was still shining feebly. Children were laughing in the next door garden. They chased each other through dripping sheets which a washer-woman was hanging from the line.

M. Grimaud arrived twenty minutes later. He heard Albert sobbing before he even opened the front door. He saw the Doctor approach as he entered the hall. He did not speak to him but went straight up to the bedroom.

The blinds were drawn. Only the light coming through the door enabled him to see the white bedspread pulled over his wife's face. He tore it away and gasped. Her mouth was open. The inside of her cheeks still gleamed with saliva.

For a moment the house was absolutely still. Albert had stopped crying since his father's arrival, and the maid who had been sobbing was silent in the kitchen. LeGrand, relieved that Grimaud seemed to be taking it so well, entered the room and put a hand on the man's shoulder as he kneeled, speechless, by the bed. Albert, also believing that his father was not reacting, walked into the hall. But his father suddenly emitted a sound between a shout and a scream. Grimaud buried his head in the bedspread which covered her breast, sobbing noiselessly between his periodic drawing of breath. He raised his head and shrugged off LeGrand's efforts to part him from the body.

When at last he did get up, he banged against the wall with his fists. He wailed, passing a hand through his hair, pulling at it again and again.

'Oh! Why did you leave me?' he cried. 'Why did you do it? Why?'

Albert and the Doctor stood watching him in the hall. He noticed them standing there. But as LeGrand approached to lead him away, he continued wailing and pulled at his collar; although it was already undone he seemed to be struggling for breath.

'Oh! Ivette my darling. How will I live without you? You were all I had. Why did you leave me? Why? Why? Why?' Again he banged his fists and pulled at his hair. His face was glistening with tears.

Albert walked into the garden. His father could see him from the landing. Almost running after his son, Grimaud seized him. He hugged him and kissed him.

'We both loved her so much.' Albert drew away. He took several steps into the darkness. 'We must be very close now. We are all alone, you and I.'

Chapter 14

Arab children were playing by the road in Chatby. They heaped dust over each other, only stopping for a moment to look at the familiar sight of a funeral procession making its way into the cemetery. A small girl, naked except for a tattered bodice, showered sand over a young mourner. She threw back her head, laughing into the late afternoon sun.

Albert scowled as he brushed the dirt from his black frock-coat. Looking away from the children, he noticed his

father crying beside him. Grimaud had wept almost con-
tinuously since his arrival home the previous evening. He
had only paused to hold his head in his hands, stunned.
Hearing his father's near-hysteria, the boy found that he
himself could remain silent. All he felt was a ghastly
sickness in his stomach.

Ahead of the moving coffin Albert saw women waiting
by the grave. His aunts' faces seemed naked in the
shadowless light; they had left off their lipstick and
mascara in mourning. The boy looked from one set of
tired features to the next without realizing that he had
passed the stone pillars which alone distinguished the
cemetery from the sandy track. He suddenly found that
the procession had halted. The coffin was laid on the
ground.

Albert's eyes met the magnified stare of an old lady
looking at him through thick, gold-rimmed spectacles.
She was almost bald. Seeing his mother's expression distorted in this, his great-Aunt Stella's face, he heard the
Rabbi intone:

'Weep with her, ye who are distressed of heart.'

Then he began going over his mother's last moments.
He had often caught himself doing so since yesterday
afternoon. It was as if he wished, though feared, to see her
gasp and grow rigid. He strained to recall the colour of her
eyes, the odour of her scent . . . All he could see now was
Aunt Stella's old face.

'May she come to her grave in peace.'

The coffin was lowered into the pit. It swayed against
the grave wall, releasing a trickle of sand. Albert remembered that earlier he and his father had each thrown a
trowel of dry earth over his mother's body. The Rabbi had
said that it had been brought from the Holy Land. Lumps
dirtied the shroud, falling against the sides of the coffin.
Grimaud reached forward to embrace the corpse. Albert
wanted to touch it also. He had refrained lest he cry like
his father.

As they recited the psalm Albert looked around him.
Faded flowers lay like weeds on the Christian tombstones.

There were no wreaths on his mother's grave; her dust would only mix with the sand.

Far off, over the flat land, the sky grew heavy with sunset. Single palms with limp branches stood in the tiring heat. Silent people in ones or twos turned to walk from the graveside. Albert stared down at the coffin long after the others had gone. Arab workmen, leaning on shovels, kept glancing towards him. They chatted and lit cigarettes. At last Grimaud came back.

'Come away now,' he said with difficulty.

Overhead, deep in its flesh-like colours, white birds travelled the streaks of the sky. Flamingos, far from their homelands, flew, extending delicate necks. Two figures, less than shadows in the evening, drew together on the fading sand. But the smaller broke away in an instant. He seemed to follow the creatures drifting with the last of the sunlight, oblivious of the deserts below.

PART IV
Four Years Later

The Desert

Chapter 15

The sand dunes seemed endless. They rose and grew and poured away, wasting into the desert. A scorching wind, tearing eddies from their surfaces, sprayed nearby mounds whose tireless motions never hardened into constant shapes. And far beyond this plain, limestone peaks overlooked the arid animation.

Albert wiped his forehead with the back of a wrist. He was crossing the surface of a rocky plateau. He glanced at the blazing landscape, but his eyes, though partially shielded by a straw hat, kept closing. Then stopping in the shade of a boulder, he shut out the desert from his vision altogether. He sighed, breathing in the suffocating air.

During the four years since his mother's death, Albert had increasingly fallen prey to turbulent moods. They seemed to overtake him without reason or warning. He might be reading, or tracing a map into an exercise book, when he would feel suddenly bored. Trailing from room to room, unable to interest himself further in whatever had completely absorbed him the moment before, he felt trapped. He longed for some undefinable freedom.

Sometimes Albert's emotions turned to anger. Outside in the yard he would pick up a stone and throw it at the opposite wall. And thrashing a clump of sugar cane without knowing why, he might go on to whip the still air with his splintering stick. On such occasions Aunt Stella watched the boy's violence from her window.

'What's wrong, darling?' she came towards him and asked. But the consolation she offered merely made Albert more inward. So without trying, or being able, to answer, he pulled away from the arm which she had drawn round his shoulder. Ambling down the village path, with its thorny plants and fibrous flowers, he told himself that a letter awaited his return. Today, as he wandered on into the surrounding desert, he anticipated a card from his father at the sanatorium in celebration of his thirteenth birthday.

Albert could remember the day, four years ago, when he had left Ramleh to stay with great-Aunt Stella. It seemed so remote that he wondered if he had ever really lived in Alexandria: perhaps the city did not exist. Gazing over the burning sand, void of all but the wind, the crowded side streets and spacious squares now appeared as strange as the smells of incense, sea, and manure which filled the corniche. The esplanade might never have been fronted by restaurants with red and green awnings, where Arabs smoked hookahs by trays of iced fish.

Everything appeared unreal on the afternoon when Aunt Stella arrived to collect Albert. (Dr. LeGrand had already dispatched the boy's father to the sanatorium. He had helped him that morning into the carriage which would take him to the train. Grimaud looked thin and white; he had hardly eaten or ventured out since his bereavement. During those three weeks he dreaded his bed at night and feared rising in the mornings. He had thanked LeGrand with a voice weak from continuous silence.) Aunt Stella and Albert whispered for some reason as they moved among furniture covered with dust-sheets. Boxes containing porcelain wrapped in old newspaper were pushed against the walls. Albert waited in the porch as Aunt Stella fumbled with the keys. Resting a hand on one of the six white pillars, he noticed that the bougainvillaea was withered; it traced round the column like straw. Lugging his suitcase down the gravel path, Albert saw a cactus flower hanging limply. The gardeners, like the servants, had long since been dismissed. Although Albert had repeatedly asked what was happening to the villa his Aunt never answered directly.

'Don't worry, darling. You'll find that everything will turn out all right in the end.'

They did not speak on the way to the station. The streets were empty except for a few beggars who had failed to escape the mid-afternoon sun. A legless man, seated in a shallow box on castors, did not even bother to extend a hand for money. Albert ignored him as he struggled past with his valise.

Normally they would have taken a cab, no matter how short the distance. His father considered it common to ride in trams. Grimaud used to send a maid to fetch a carriage. And he would have expected the driver to arrange the luggage, especially in this heat. But Aunt Stella, with her black dress and glass earrings, assumed that they would wait for the tram. She picked out the smallest coins from her purse when the conductor asked for their fares.

The vehicle lurched away from Boulevard Ramleh. They were running parallel to the sea. All the way down the straight coast line the avenues of palms were filling with drowsy Europeans and shopkeepers, strolling after their siestas. Although people moved slowly, they seemed to jerk past the wooden frame of Albert's window. The images kept disappearing into the mist which his breath had made on the glass. He wiped away the opaque moisture. Through his fingers he saw the back of their house. Yet the white villa with its winding staircase and tall cypresses grew cloudy. By the time he cleaned the pane, Ramleh was left far behind.

Their train went westwards from Alexandria. It would eventually lead far beyond their destination, to el Alamein. Albert could still make out the sea from behind the half-desert through which they were travelling. It seemed rosy in the declining sun. But then, as they began turning eastwards, they came upon a long sea of salt. It gleamed in the last of the light and grew dull as evening broke. Stars crystallized over the desert. Breezes shifted stray fragments of clouds. At one point, on a hill far from the city, Albert saw the jagged ruins of a house.

Albert did not know how long it would be before he returned to Alexandria, or when he would see his father again. All he could say was that something vital had faded with the home he remembered, that few things would be the same again. Yet while he thought the house shimmered in his mind as though through dark waters. He was back with his parents, harmonious and relaxed.

Albert remembered watching his mother arranging flowers in the early evening; everything should be perfect for her husband's return. The dining-table reflected the scarlet petals, while Mme Grimaud played the piano and listened for the door. Occasionally she looked up and lifted her fingers from the keys. Gently putting a hand to the back of her head and adjusting her hair, she listened, thinking that her Solomon had just entered.

Albert looked before him at the person with whom he would now be living. He noticed again the similarity between Aunt Stella's mouth and his mother's. The movement of the train had jogged her head towards the window. Moonlight was blanching her cheek.

Away in the darkness, the wind scattered the sand. Like dead seeds it blew away from the dunes, only to fall on parched land. Albert wondered who lived here. How did they survive among the salt and the rock? Remembering the sand to which all were consigned at Chatby, he flinched in anticipation of his own desert home.

For a sudden moment he could not accept that his mother's warmth had departed. Surely her jokes and embraces would continue unchanged. She would sit on his bed every evening, telling stories of her childhood and parents. And her presence, so unquestionable, with its associations of perfumes and parties, how could it have been transformed into that of a frightened invalid? Worse still, how had a patient been succeeded, with hardly a word of explanation, by the strange old lady, dressed in withered clothes, who was leading him into the desert?

THE DESERT

Standing in the train's draughty passage, Albert recoiled from the agitation which these thoughts had provoked. He shuddered at a momentary impression that the vehicle was carrying him, its only passenger, through a tunnel leading into the earth. Having no wish to consider the images of starlessness which seized hold of his mind, Albert found himself deploying all his ingenuity in making things other than they were.

Might his mother not simply be in a coma, unconscious, not really dead? Or maybe she was only pretending, playing a cruel joke at his expense. As he rejected each possibility, his ideas became more far-fetched. Albert no longer believed his own inventions. He knew that this was not a dream. Resting against the window, looking into the darkness, he finally admitted to himself that his mother was dead. He had first really seen it when he had entered the room containing her coffin. Her face had been insensibly peaceful. Her body would never be reclaimed from the sand.

For a while, once he accepted the fact, Albert stared without focusing his vision. His body submitted to the vibrations of the train. Soon he felt faint and could not even recall what he had been considering. He had returned to his carriage, indifferent to the other passenger.

Standing now in the desert, four years later, he felt equally numbed. He yawned in the inadequate shade of the boulder. Before him, stretching away in the unbearable heat, he saw the same desert through which he had travelled on that afternoon and evening. He had seen it countless times since. He always rested at this spot. It provided the only alternative to Aunt Stella's house and the village.

At first Albert had rarely left his new home. He preferred to sit in the half-light, soon disposing of homework which he found far below the standard he had already attained with his tutors. His room, like the others, was fitted with irregular scraps of carpet. These brownish rugs were faded and frayed; lengths of string fell away from their ends.

More than once Albert saw Aunt Stella crawling around on a piece of mat.

'Now where did I put them? I know I put them somewhere.' She would be talking to herself, not seeming to realize that Albert had just returned from school. She lifted cushions, emptied her handbag, and even peered into the lavatory. 'I really must find them. I'm as blind as a bat without my glasses.'

Recently Albert refused to join the search. He was now used to his Aunt's absent-mindedness. He knew that she would mislay her spectacles at some stage of the day. Only when he saw the old lady approach him on all fours, would he bend down and draw the glasses from the crown of her head to her eyes.

'Oh! it's you! Thank God! I thought you'd never come back.' She would kiss Albert again and again.

Several days ago he had observed that face, so reminiscent of another, wince in terror as her fingers touched an apparently alien boot. Without understanding his impulse to intensify her fear into frenzy, Albert refrained from announcing that it was he who stood before her. Seconds later, but only once his cruelty became too disturbing to him, he placed her spectacles on the bridge of her nose.

Soon after, Aunt Stella went to her bedroom to rest. She was trembling more than usual. Yet even in her absence Albert could not stop thinking of her lying in darkness. He wished he could rid himself of the thought as he turned to his study.

Finishing his homework Albert gathered up his books and replaced the sheets of newspaper which usually covered the surface of his table.

'We must protect the furniture from dust. It gets very dusty out here,' Aunt Stella had explained to her great-nephew on his arrival. 'Of course,' she added, fingering the top page of a journal, 'your mother was used to a beautiful house.' Her eyes carried on the expression, half wistful and half apologetic, of her voice.

As it happened, the newspapers proved more useful than

Aunt Stella had suspected. For when the lanky school-master, a young man in whose features all the races of the Levant seemed to unite, had been discoursing on recent French history several months ago, Albert contradicted him with facts which had been news twenty years previously. The other pupils in the small European class were delighted by the aplomb with which their bespectacled teacher was confused. Accordingly, Albert invested in their hero worship by reading a supplementary pile of yellowing newspapers. Removing the sheet with which Aunt Stella shrouded the armchairs, and laying aside the cushion in order to preserve the sandy stains which passed as 'gold braid', he released whole colonies of insects while he sat inspecting the pages.

By now Albert's classmates laughed at almost anything he said. Although he enjoyed their ready adulation it surprised him that they should be amused by his serious remarks. Then, at the end of a morning even more riotous than the rest, the master removed his glasses, perpetually misted of late. Rubbing his naked eyelids with a gesture eloquent of approaching middle age, he issued a stern ultimatum for the benefit of the *agent provocateur* in their midst. Albert was shocked at being treated so unjustly. He was piqued by the public humiliation. Worse than either was the instantaneous withdrawal of his admirers' support. If only he could have remained in the care of his private tutors!

Hours after school ended, Albert exiled himself to the front porch, together with his homework. He had no desire to meet the others as usual. They seemed childish and gross. Nor did he care to answer his Aunt when she asked:

'Aren't you too hot here? Why don't you go out with your friends?'

He continued writing, only looking up when a breeze set dry leaves trembling in their pots. Before him a black dog of no particular breed cocked a leg, its outline golden in the intense light. The mongrel urinated against a wall and passed beyond the few Europeans' houses. They were made of brick and soft timber; grey sheets and restless pigeons filled their flat roofs. The animal continued down the main path, nosing its way through the rotten fruit and offal. On either side dense clouds of flies hovered near the entrances of Arab huts. The insects barely dispersed when the dog strayed into the manure to which they were attracted. Albert looked further on. Even the patches of onions and bitter herbs, which the peasants cultivated so assiduously, seemed like a species of sand. A fellah shielded his eyes from the sun as he led a blindfolded buffalo in circles round a well. Hearing barking, Albert turned back and watched the dog run down the rest of the track. It came upon some of his classmates by the mud pool which supplied the village's building materials.

The others were running by the edge, chasing one another, throwing stones and lumps of earth.

'The barbarians!' Albert thought as a piece of wood hit a younger boy on the elbow and forced him, agonized, to the ground. When the child recovered, minutes later, he looked for the small Arab who had hurled the piece of timber. Getting up he ran over, then attacked him with a fistful of sand. But the Arab's cousin, one of several peasant youths who had been excluded from the pupils' activities, crept over behind the boy. He pushed him and dragged him by the wrists into the pool.

The child thrashed about in the foul-smelling liquid, screaming insults at the spectators. Then raising himself until he was only waist-deep in slime, he sprayed the onlookers with mud. Climbing out, crying with fury, he picked up a bamboo. He split it by beating the air.

Albert gritted his teeth at the jeers which the boy excited. Yet soon the child himself was laughing. He brought his stick down on the dog. He pushed it into the pool. Thereafter a succession of people joined the mongrel.

As each new person landed in the pit—and some danced at its very edge shamelessly soliciting the shove required to topple their balance—the boy would jump up and down, daring a friend to enter the slime. If need be he climbed out and dragged him, protesting with giggles, back with him. After wallowing about for a time, both would return to the sand. With their caking of mud Albert could not tell victor and victim apart; he did not know which were Arabs and which Europeans.

The sun was setting. Huts cast long shadows on the sand. Yet the pit was still filled with bodies. Others ran and squatted at its side. Albert told himself that he had no desire to know the others. They were no better than Arabs themselves. The hero worship of near-savages was worthless. He had no need of their admiration or support.

By now those who had only watched the various tussles submitted to the pool of their own accord. Some drew themselves to the edge of the pit on their bellies and simply flopped into the mire. Others, recently raised from the slime, crawled about spraying their muddy bodies with sand.

Albert found everybody unrecognizable. There was even barking from within one clayey form. Was there any difference between them and animals? They were all on all fours.

Albert was still watching long after the sun set. Strange earth shapes seemed to be absorbed into the dark desert. They were gathered into the body of night.

It was only after some time that Albert left the front porch. He was disturbed by the constant grating of crickets; he shivered in the cool wind. Getting up to clear away his homework, he noticed a baby crying. He had heard the sound previously but remained unaware of it until now.

For some reason the incident overwhelmed him. It remained with him even though its participants had gone home. Their forms, disturbing and hostile, multiplied in his mind. While he visualized them coupling, fusing, and releasing each other in the warm sand, he was scarcely conscious that it was he, Albert Grimaud, who was thinking. It seemed as if the flesh and bones containing his perceptions had inexplicably faded. He was open to frightening but covert sensations; they neither bore the impression of the world he knew, nor of himself.

Albert remembered that when he was younger he had always lived life regardless of the fact that he was himself. As he coloured a picture or swam he had been absorbed by the paint or the sea. In those days he rarely thought of the past and the future. If he did, they seemed like pleasant or unpleasant hallucinations which were only incidentally real. Yet recently, far from being in the thrall of the present, he disdained each moment before it had passed. His life, rather than following the progress of time like his heartbeats, trailed after nebulous moods. He lived in pursuit of the role, the existence, which the relief of anxiety required.

Leaving the porch, Albert began to consider the muddy forms with greater detachment. These boys, he told himself, were unworthy of his attention; they were common and banal. But although he rehearsed the reasons, social and intellectual, for dissociating himself from his classmates, he never successfully banished the disturbing memory of their recent activities. And the pit, claiming each for its slime, seemed even more vivid. Simply thinking of it made him grow dizzy. He felt as if he were sinking when he lay down.

It was not the first time that Albert had been so agitated. He occasionally stood still, sweating, with darkness before his eyes. Sometimes he found himself short of breath, his pulse racing. It was the kind of panic he knew when other boys exchanged pieces of information about how babies were born. (He often wished that he had never been given the fascinating reason why adults slept in the same bed.) Yet he had experienced these sensations more frequently during the last few months since the incident at the pool.

Albert was almost swooning now as he rested by the desert boulder. Looking beyond the pocket of shade in which he was standing, his eyelids kept sinking. The sand appeared to have changed to a lighter element; it glowed, fiery, through the heavy flaps of skin. After a moment he was seeing black patches. Then everything was dark.

These evenings, Albert reflected, there were only

shadows. Aunt Stella had recently taken to sitting with her grand-nephew after dinner. They would sip Turkish coffee without lighting the lamp. A voice from a neighbouring house echoed in the room. It was so piercing that their little cups would rattle in the saucers. Eventually there would be silence.

Aunt Stella would say nothing. She merely stirred an empty cup, nodding in the darkness. From time to time Albert thought she was about to speak; he might incline his head towards her. But watching her lips continue moving without uttering a sound, he realized that she was simply trembling.

Albert found it taxing to sit still while his great-Aunt gazed purposelessly through the small window. He too might look at the drab houses opposite. Yet he would suddenly feel that he was being sucked down a dark well. His stomach floated as it did when he seemed to be falling in dreams . . . He would rise and suggest that they light the oil lamp. Aunt Stella might say that they would in a minute. Albert had known her to fail to answer altogether. He would have to go on sitting in silence for what seemed like an endless period of time before asking again about the light. He stopped himself from looking at the clock for as long as he could. Finally he peeped: only a few minutes would have passed.

Once, when Albert had offered to light the lamp for a second time, Aunt Stella had not replied. He repeated his suggestion but she still did not answer. Heavy whiffs of garbage were riding in on the stifling air.

'Aunt Stella!' Her chin had dropped over onto one shoulder. The furry hemisphere, with which she usually contrived to hide her balding scalp, slipped over her forehead. 'Aunt Stella!' A strange buzzing filled Albert's head. He knew that it had not entered his ears. The muscles in his neck tautened; his fists clenched; his entire body grew contorted. 'Aunt Stella!' He felt as if he were suffocating in the dark foul-smelling room. Alone with that face, deadened by lunar light . . . Aunt Stella yawned and looked blankly around her.

'My goodness! I must have dropped off.'

They were sitting together again a few evenings later. This time the lamp had been lit. It sighed as Aunt Stella interspersed her conversation with reminiscences.

'You're growing up now. Soon you'll be a young gentleman. You should be going to parties where you can meet young ladies of your own age.' Albert was looking out of the window at the dusty track and mud houses. Was it conceivable that he would ever be invited to such a function?

'Parties,' Aunt Stella said. 'It's only natural.' She was almost talking to herself now. 'I remember such wonderful parties. Your mother was a great hostess. I still remember her coming to our house at your age. Of course she wasn't so serious.' Aunt Stella went on stirring her coffee. It was as though she thereby generated images from the past in that portion of space into which she was staring. 'Everyone used to think she was pretty. She had a very fair complexion, which is unusual. And she had such a lovely personality. So sweet.'

Still stirring, she did not realize that Albert had left the room.

'Of course, we lived in Ramleh in those days. That was before your great-Uncle lost his money. We had a villa with a beautiful garden. There was every kind of tree you can imagine; palm trees, acacia trees, carob trees, eucalyptus trees. And such grass! Not like this.' She looked around her. Where was her nephew? The spoon grew still in the chipped cup.

Albert had wandered to the edge of the village. He stood by the mud pit, looking into the darkness. A breeze blowing off the desert chilled his bare arms. It seemed to carry away something of his life with the sand. Lately all had felt barren to Albert. There was no alleviation for his terrible boredom; no relief for the meaningless sequence of his days. Yet while he had dreamt of Ramleh, gazing into the wilderness, while Aunt Stella drank her evening coffee, now, days later in the shade of a boulder, such thoughts appeared futile. For seeing the white light breaking up into spectrums, he dismissed his memories as over-colourful. Besides, memories invariably faded with the approach of his darker moods.

Suddenly there was a flash in the distance. Albert moved his head to look more closely. There! It glittered again. He supposed it might be the sun catching on a ship's canvas. He imagined a clipper sailing the oceans. A breeze would be stirring the rigging, cool and heavy with spray. Rising and falling with each wave, the sea dispersed in sheets at his sides. He was floating freely like the clouds, forgetting the heat, the voices, the faces . . .

Nothing moved in the desert except sand and his shadow. There was the glinting of a far-off rock. It shimmered like the surrounding peaks. The silver fleck remained in Albert's mind although he had recognized that it was limestone. It grew, as luminous things sometimes did, inflaming his imagination. It released inexhaustible desires; it filled him with a sense of anticipation. He even enjoyed a momentary feeling of power. There was nothing he could not achieve.

Startling impulses often hovered on the threshold of Albert's consciousness. They might sally forth in the company of vivid images. He would be on the verge of grasping such forms, yet they always withdrew in a matter of moments. He could lay hold on nothing more tangible than moods.

Now he felt cool, as if he were in a large room with wide windows. He could not be sure if there was a marble floor. He sensed an air of unobtrusive decorum: silent servants crossing spacious halls. Perhaps too there was that suppressed excitement associated with palaces, an atmosphere of momentous decisions and impending events. Ormolu mirrors reflected ancestral portraits hanging along the whole lengths of galleries.

It seemed to Albert that he himself was the occasion of this splendour. He was vaguely aware that the richness emanated from him. A symphony, solemn as a hymn, swelled in praise of his greatness. Like a monarch he stood at the centre of universal acclamation.

Thrilling to the idea of himself as an emperor, Albert noticed that his thinking was less inhibited than before. He found that he could pursue sensations and images further; they ultimately touched on memories and places he knew. The gracious palace, of which he had previously received only an intimation, now assumed the form of his father's house. His diffused impression of its chambers, galleries, and hallways settled into a distinct picture of Grimaud's study. The statuette of Bonaparte, the Empire furniture, the framed map of a successful desert campaign —these, together with Napoleon's beloved *Lives* by Plutarch, held pride of place in the room.

Albert had always associated the Emperor with his father. Indeed they had been so linked in his mind as a small boy that he had assumed that Napoleon *was* his father, though different. Understanding nothing of the man's historical existence, how could Albert suppose that Bonaparte was other than a version of the only male adult with whom he was familiar?

Albert had not only made the Emperor's acquaintance through the furnishings in Grimaud's study. He remembered painting Bonaparte's face in a colouring book his father had once given him. And Albert often lay on the floor listening to stories about the great hero. Grimaud was usually content to forget his son, break off the stories, and carry on their dry subject matter in boring conversations with guests. Yet although Albert had long connected Napoleon with his father, he recently thought of the Emperor—as a minute before—more as the embodiment of his own aspirations than as a vehicle for recalling his parent.

Albert could now see that he had actually created a second Napoleon, a hero very different from his father's Bonaparte. Of course he had frequently been suspicious of the shining example of virtue held out to him in childhood. Who but a collaborator with grown-ups would have allowed his Imperial style to be invoked as an exemplum of the success purchased by hard work? Nevertheless, Albert had been hardly aware of the development of another Napoleon at the outset; his Emperor's characteristics had been entirely negative at first.

Albert's Bonaparte, no matter what had been recorded of his life, was not squeamish about being touched.

'Stop putting your dirty fingers there,' M. Grimaud said as his son followed the statuette's profile with hands sticky with toffee. Nor was his Napoleon susceptible to influenza.

'Look at me!' Albert once said as he marched through the hall, dressed in nothing but a towel for a toga. 'I'm an Emperor.'

'You're nothing of the sort. Go and finish your bath before you catch a cold.'

Now, looking back to those times, Albert could see that his Napoleon was quite simply the opposite of his father's. His hero would have no truck with ideals such as obedience, will-power, and unstinted effort. Merely naming them recalled to Albert the tyranny under which he had seemed to pass his childhood. Nor would he antagonize invalids, interrogate boys, utter self-righteous homilies, shout, come to blows. The memory subsided as if it had been a wave of nausea.

Albert's Napoleon was not even an expressionless bust. He did not hide under a sheet in the way that Grimaud had shut himself off in his study. Simply visualizing the statuette's cheeks, cool to the touch, and its chiselled nostrils and eyes, carried him across the years. It reminded him of his father's photograph album in which details or facial expressions were clear enough to suggest that the pictures had been taken only the day before, whereas the inescapable atmosphere of each snapshot hinted at a greater passage of time. No. Albert's Napoleon was neither distant nor cold. He hardly even enjoyed an external existence. He was as near to the boy as he was to himself. More: he lived and grew in areas which Albert could scarcely conceive of. He inspired the boy's deepest desires. He gave him the courage to entertain passionate hopes.

Suddenly, as a minute ago almost glimpsing the ship,

Albert would become aware of new energies. They filled him with a feeling of strength; he was equal to any challenge. And his life, once purposeless and drab, beckoned him onto ever greater achievements. Obstacles would fall away at his feet; there were no hurdles, no doors left unopened. Other people could be left to struggle with the infirmities of their limited world. He despised them for their fear and ordinariness.

Albert was now conscious of another image. His father had been sitting on the sofa shortly after his wife's death. He was silent, red eyed, and still; an arm hung in his lap, curiously limp. The Doctor, having observed M. Grimaud's state for several days, regretfully suggested that he be sent to Professor Valence's sanatorium. Then, shepherding the boy out of the room, LeGrand looked at the ground.

'Em . . . Albert, em . . . You mustn't feel ashamed.' He had seemed almost furtive. 'These things sometimes happen . . . And above all, don't feel ashamed.' He had moved off without looking at Albert.

They happened sometimes perhaps, but Albert would never let such a thing happen to him! His strength of will was too great. He at least would remain firm.

Albert jerked forward. He felt dizzy; he was going to faint. Reaching out for the boulder the ground seemed to rise. Everything grew dark. He was falling, and falling.

As he put out a hand to help himself up, Albert found the sand scorching, though shaded. He must return to the village at once. After all, he was expecting a card from his father. He anticipated walking into his room and seeing the envelope lying on his bed. The thought might help obliterate his growing panic. He feared collapsing with sun stroke before reaching home. Nobody would find him. He would dry into dust.

He looked before him: there was sand. There was sand at each side. He turned back. The boulder loomed up. Beyond he saw desert.

Chapter 16

Pierre LeGrand had always intended to visit M. Grimaud at the sanatorium. Over the last four years he answered his ex-patient's doleful messages, communicated to him by nuns leaving their work at the hospital to return to the order in Alexandria, with notes saying that he hoped to see him in the near future. Yet the Doctor's pressure of work always prevented him from making the trip.

Perhaps too the political troubles made him wary of leaving his flat unattended. Anyone could climb in by breaking the lavatory window. Certainly he felt some hesitation at going out of the city; he had heard of Europeans being attacked on trains. Besides the sanatorium was some way off in the desert. And supposing he were to make the arduous journey, what would he be likely to find?

Probably he was also deterred by an atavistic fear of such institutions and their inmates, a limitation, he realized, in a member of his profession. His memories of a grown man like Grimaud reduced to paroxysms of grief and child-like dependence were still too vivid for him to seek contact with the deranged. So recently, hearing that M. Grimaud was feeling much better, the obstacles in the way of a visit seemed less important. The Doctor felt he needed a change of air. He would go to the sanatorium for a week-end.

LeGrand could not have been more pleasantly surprised when he arrived. M. Grimaud was as finely dressed that morning as he used to be in the days when they walked on the lawn at Ramleh. His snugly fitting white coat was surmounted by a powder-blue cravat and pearl tie-pin. His beard was so well trimmed that he could have just walked out of the barber's shop in the Hotel Cecil. He smiled, shook LeGrand warmly by the hand, said how delighted he was to see him, and produced a bottle of champagne.

They drank it sitting in wickerwork chairs, exchanging

prepared though friendly superficialities on the veranda. Honeysuckle and jasmine trailed over the walls. A fountain nourished miniature irrigation canals; the channels carried precious water to brilliant red flowers with petals as large as tongues. They stretched away, row upon row, up to palms whose outer branches hung over the desert.

Relaxing in the sunshine, his head swimming delightfully, LeGrand almost thought himself on holiday in a villa. He could only marvel at the skill with which the institution's function had been disguised with whitewash and subtropical foliage. While the nuns, tracing through the colonnades, seemed as remote as peacocks with their fantastic coifs.

LeGrand might never have noticed the way in which Grimaud had begun picking at his cuticles had the noonday light not forced him to glance away from the garden. He could have remained ignorant of the pained and distant expression which had gradually settled on his face. But then Grimaud started speaking in a precise, disjointed manner. The Doctor remembered the tone from his ex-patient's previous attempts to organize sudden, almost overwhelming emotions.

'I often sit here in the mornings . . . Between the flowers you can see the sand . . . I remember going to the desert with my father.'

There were long pauses between the sentences, periods in which Grimaud stared into the distance. Accustomed to solitude, he was now perhaps unaware of, or even indifferent to, the Doctor's presence. Yet once, when LeGrand waved aside a fly, Grimaud's knuckles whitened about one arm of his chair. The other hand was lifeless in his lap.

Grimaud's voice, deliberately steadied at first, was growing more even. Running a hand over his beard, he looked at LeGrand and went on:

'Have I told you about my father before? No? Oh! That's right. I must have spoken to Professor Valence.' Grimaud looked into the distance. 'I'll never forget the way my father used to be at his documents by six o'clock in the morning, every morning. I remember him sitting, hardly able to breathe. His asthma gave him terrible insomnia . . . I suffer from insomnia too.' He went on as if he had never mentioned himself; the reference might have been to his father. 'My father had such a strong will that he virtually made our cotton business into an empire. And when I "joined" the firm'—he screwed up his eyes as if to question his choice of the word—'he expected me to work as hard as he did. My brother too. I remember getting over a bout of food poisoning once. He came into my bedroom and said that if he could work with all his illnesses I certainly could.' Grimaud was half-laughing but the Doctor, not knowing whether he should be impressed or shocked by the father's behaviour, suppressed any reaction. 'I got up there and then, though I could hardly stand, and went straight to the office. "You're just like the old man," the clerks said. They were afraid of him too. He ruled us all with an iron fist. I was "just like the old man".' The Doctor felt sure that Grimaud must be repeating it to himself. His arm hung useless, paralysed. 'And now this.' A cheek and lower eyelid quivered.

Lunch was served in Grimaud's room. They sat at a small table.

'What will you do when you leave?' LeGrand asked.

'I've been thinking about that. I don't think I'll go back into the business. I'd like to sell the firm, or at least let my manager go on running it for me.' He put down his napkin, having hardly touched the food. Lighting a cigar, he watched the dense smoke curl into the air. It floated through the window, over the garden, and into the desert. 'I don't want to go on as before. What I was doing in Alexandria was nearly stifling me. I felt buried alive out there.' He looked beyond the veranda at the sand. It stretched as far as the sky. 'Somehow I didn't realize it at the time. It seems almost incredible now, but that's just being wise after the event. I suppose I must have been afraid,' he sighed, 'or something.'

Later that afternoon they walked in the garden. Flowers were casting long shadows.

'I imagine you'll feel rather bored if you don't do something.' (LeGrand was recalling that his evening surgery
usually started at this time, as he gazed into the vast
spaces.)

'I shall think for some time. Being here has helped me in
that. You know, in the past I believed that I should always
be active, doing something: business, letters, it didn't
matter what. Now I see how much I missed—' he broke
off his sentence hearing a piano being played. 'That must
be Professor Valence. You really should meet him. He's
quite——' Again he sacrificed his words to the notes
drifting over the flowers.

'My wife used to play,' he continued. 'Of course in those
days I never listened.' He pulled the head off a poppy as he
mentioned her. Discarding the petals, one by one, he
watched the fragments of colour float down and join their
shadows on the sand.

'I remember hearing her play as I came home in the
evenings. But my head was too full of other things. Ivette
even taught Albert to play . . .' He stopped, preoccupied,
almost smiling. Perhaps he was remembering the mother
with her child. 'I wonder if he still practises.'

Grimaud continued talking about Albert as they walked
on. 'He's never answered any of my letters. But then I
suppose he thinks I rather ignored him. Things were very
difficult for me then.' He added it as if in self-defence.
LeGrand was looking at his shoes, nodding his head very
slightly. 'I know it can't have been easy for a boy of nine.
I just hope he hasn't become ashamed. Do you think he *is*
ashamed——?'

'No. I can't see why.' The Doctor only looked up to
glance away into the distance.

'Still, I don't suppose I shall be here for much longer,'
Grimaud said, trying to alter the mood of the conversation with a burst of enthusiasm. 'The moment I get
settled again in Ramleh he can come home.' But as they
passed the fountain, now dead, on their way back to his
room, Grimaud muttered, perplexed: 'Sometimes he could
be so strange.'

'Yes. He doesn't want anyone to know what's going on in his head,' LeGrand volunteered, weakly trying to convert the father's observation into a compliment. 'I shouldn't be surprised if he does something important in his life.'

'Maybe. His grandfather was a great man. He might follow in his footsteps. But,' his silhouette was softened by the advancing darkness, 'I don't think he should become too ruthless. If he does he'll be terribly lonely.'

LeGrand had been invited to meet Professor Valence after dinner. The Mother Superior came to fetch him from Grimaud's room. She spoke just above a whisper and with very few words. The Doctor was surprised that she was not older. She preceded him down the corridor by several steps. At regular intervals he saw her white habit illumined by a dense arc of light. As she passed on, the lamp was reflected by tiles.

The Mother Superior led him, without turning back, across a patio and down further passages. She once encountered a nun; neither greeted the other. Only on approaching a small house did she slacken her swift, imperturbable pace. She signalled the half-open door, and withdrew without speaking.

Professor Valence was sitting alone in the candle-lit study. From the moment he looked up at the visitor, LeGrand found his eyes inescapable. They seemed like opals through whose impassive surfaces there glowed the innumerable colours of a constant inner energy. As he spoke he would raise the dome of his forehead, his grey hair swept back from his face, and stare beyond LeGrand. Then gazing past the mirrors, dulled by dimness, he came upon indistinct bronze forms from which his lighted expression appeared to mould new sentiments and meanings. Yet somewhere in his voice, in the tone by which LeGrand could tell he wished to speak of almost sacred things, there was a sense of groping, as if he made his way towards each word through darkness and with difficulty. Sometimes, lifting his head for minutes at a time and searching the vacant air, the Doctor imagined that Valence sought to penetrate an opaque film, stretched across his eyes like scales, and see with total clearness.

'I am, perhaps, Tiresias,' he said. The spaces above both cheeks were hollowed out by shadow. 'They had no wish to hear me when I was practising in Paris. You see, we French like everything to be so clear. Lucidity and Reason!' He almost smiled. 'Beside these virtues surely there is nothing! And yet the world is not so clear. And if you say that we are all a little blind, they'll send you, like a madman, to this desert. If only fools could be made rational again, I heard them say, their madness will depart. Mesmerism, opiates, correction, hydrotherapy, windy passageways and halls: use these, and so dispel the darkness that blots out the brilliant light of reason. If you should answer that the world *is* dark, and that the darkest sky of all is that in which the distant rational star is thought to shine, they'll say that you have lost your mind; that you are blind, like your patients. And yet,' LeGrand saw the Professor raise an index finger, 'and yet, hold to the darkness of which we are made, the darkness which is fastened to the rich fluid that gives us life, and you shall find treasures immeasurable. In our dreams, in our desires, in the recesses of our cavernous selves, there lie those prophesies of wholeness of which each one of us alone is his own oracle. How to interpret the signs?' Valence went on, knitting his brow. ' "How to interpret them?" This is the question I have always been trying to answer. Of course it is different for different individuals. People in distress, like your old patient Solomon Grimaud, seem to be so haunted by their anxieties that they are driven on, by God knows what, to find what answers they can. And yet, how can I ever know that they have been successful? There are occasions, maybe now,' he glanced at the Doctor, 'when I wonder if my life's work has been wasted. After all, what do I do? Sometimes Grimaud and I talk. Usually he reflects, walks and reflects. He suffers a little, at nights no doubt a great deal. There are some patients who will never recover. Others might have done so without ever coming here.' His head fell low, lost in the shadows. 'And beneath it all, I feel I'm struggling in the darkness like them.'

The Doctor could not see Grimaud's face as he entered his bedroom sometime after. Though his head lay sleeping on the pillow, its outlines seemed to have been diffused into the night.

'Who can tell,' he remembered Valence saying, 'what gives one person the courage to descend into the darkness, rather than another? What enables this man and not that to search the awful vacancy to meet some stranger self? It is impossible to say, after all, if I shall eventually shed those features inherited from my father in favour of a truer "me". We cannot will the courage, or the insight. We are fated to be mere fishermen casting our nets in endlessly capricious waters. This is, is it not?' and here he smiled again, 'a splendid curse.'

Book Two

PART I
Four Years Later

A Race

Chapter 1

The sea was turbulent all the way along the coastline. Its greyish waves were forced from their regular motions by a cold wind which drove them sideways to the shore. There they broke open, falling backwards from the impact. They spilled their white spray onto the sand. Even the movement of a steamship, heading for harbour, seemed distorted as its taper of smoke was caught up into the racing clouds. It sailed in a wide arc, passing a gunboat anchored beyond the dock limits. A red, white, and blue flag hung from the motionless vessel; it looked like laundry, limp in the interminable rain.

Daniel Benchimol lit a cigar as he looked at the port from his top floor sitting-room. All around him he could see, superimposed on this European part of the city, his own figure gazing out of the Hotel Cecil; it was reflected in the fluid mirrors made up of red roof tiles and deepening pools of rain. Beyond the houses and shops, concealed beneath his image, ran a belt of mud huts. It neither glistened nor shimmered. It took his eye, never returning its glance, down to the harbour and sea.

The steamship had now come into port. Arabs, clustering beneath umbrellas, newspapers, baskets, and each others' *gallabiyas*, surged forward from the shelter of the customs shed, as the gangplank was lowered. With their wares—handbags, brass trays, peanuts, deformities, carriages—they jostled the emerging passengers.

Several days ago Daniel had walked off a similar gang-plank. It had seemed, he remembered, as if scores of hands were competing for his luggage. The cases were scrutinized by even more pairs of eyes. Carrying the valises himself along the slippery quayside, barely able to see through his misted spectacles, he longed for a free hand with which to inspect the wallet he hoped his inside pocket would still contain.

During those last few years in Lyons Daniel had almost forgotten the suspicion one grew to feel towards everyone in Alexandria. He scarcely spared a thought for the unspeakable things; urine sold as cologne, barbers shaving clients with razors that transmitted skin diseases, Arabs who blew their noses in their hands and used walls as handkerchiefs. But on his arrival he had suddenly been reminded. For, unable to carry his valises a step further without stopping, he found that he had acquired a porter while he stood cleaning his glasses. Daniel had been forced to follow the luggage which was marched on several paces ahead.

Now, two days later, Benchimol opened his hotel window. A mouthful of cigar smoke dispersed in the grey atmosphere. Before him, in the harbour, Egyptians still scuttled about the mass of Europeans. Their voices were silenced by the distance and rain.

He recalled having passed a middle-aged passenger, clearly more irascible or foolish than he. The short man, stout in a white suit which the rain reduced to a tailored sheet, was running behind two Arab youths. He was screaming incomprehensibly as they carried off his battered luggage. At one point he almost caught them up: he tried to lay hold on their *gallabiyas*. But Daniel saw one of the would-be porters turn, pull at the breathless passenger's outstretched arm, and throw him to the ground. The man simply remained there, shouting, his clothes covered in mud. Then, nursing his balding head, he began groaning and sobbing. When he looked up into the pouring rain his cheeks and temples were dirty.

Daniel remembered that the other passengers had now

been pouring into the customs shed. A ship's horn was hooting. Even the Arabs who had previously ignored the weather, preferred shelter to the few piastres they might make as porters.

The man was still lying on the quayside; he called out weakly, trying to prop himself up on an elbow, hugging one side. But the rain had grown worse, and although some people like Daniel stopped for a moment to look back, it seemed that there was nothing they could do. Besides, they were forced on into the shed by the porters carrying their luggage.

At last the young Arabs returned with the valises. They looked down at the groaning man. He tried to shout; with considerable effort he raised himself onto one knee. They allowed him to struggle, as if in pity. Then seeing him raise his flabby body almost to its full height, one spilled the contents of the luggage on the mud. The other pushed him over, kicking the side of his face.

Daniel was watching from the entrance of the shed. The Arab kicked again and again. In the second between the youths' pausing to look down and running off in the other direction, the body winced and grew still. Daniel recalled the noise of passengers moving through customs . . .

Benchimol was jerked out of his reverie by the bell of the Anglican Church. As he listened he noticed himself anticipating each of its tolls. And when the clock started striking he found that he was counting aloud:

'—two—three—four—five.' The bell, the clock, and Daniel fell silent. The disagreeable memory was almost dispelled.

Daniel's words were the first he had spoken for over an hour. They sounded dead in the dismal light, among this sombre hotel furniture. If he could have read, or written letters, he might have ignored his surroundings. Yet waiting for a note to be delivered to his room, he paced to and from the window. At any moment the messenger might knock.

At least he had been able to sit still yesterday at this hour. Daniel had been taking tea with Pierre LeGrand, downstairs in the foyer. He had known, even before leaving Lyons, that the Doctor would insist that the ceremony be revived during his visit to the city. He visualized the conversation flagging after the initial affirmations of friendship.

'How are things now in Alexandria?' Daniel asked after the first major silence. They had talked of private matters hitherto.

'Much the same as usual, I suppose. Sometimes things seem to get better,' the Doctor touched the fingertips of one hand to those of the other, 'but then . . .' He finished the sentence with his hands falling away like a house of cards. 'Of course it's the same in life——'

'—Has there been much violence?' Daniel wished to avoid the morose tone which the Doctor's last remark threatened to introduce into the conversation. It might have led to a self-pitying description of LeGrand's loneliness, and stimulated tacit reproaches of his young friend for returning to France. After all, LeGrand had tried to dissuade Benchimol from leaving Egypt four years ago.

'Violence?' The Doctor looked over one shoulder, almost startled. He turned back immediately his eyes met the coy glance of a thin, middle-aged lady suffering from a goitre; she was adding more slices of lemon to her tea. 'Well, things are always rather tense here.' He touched his birthmark and stared into the distance. 'But apart from that, there's nothing.' He continued stroking the mulberry cheek.

'So Europeans haven't been attacked?' Daniel scarcely believed that the news of his fellow passenger's murder could by-pass the Doctor. Even the theft of a pin would be common knowledge among the foreign community.

'I expect there have been *some* incidents.' LeGrand was surely positively blushing. Daniel found it difficult to understand why he should feign ignorance of the event. Of course LeGrand had always been weak; he invariably feared being assaulted. Doubtless when he was confronted by actual danger his cowardice, previously engaged in manufacturing spectres, would be employed in distorting unpleasant reality.

'Yes, everything seems much quieter than a few years ago.' Daniel now felt unaccountably nervous. He thought that the Doctor was observing him, though he did not turn to verify his impression.

'The only incident I've heard of,' LeGrand went on, 'took place at the docks. A man was kicked to death, or so I've been told.' Benchimol did not reply. He was sure that the Doctor expected to elicit a remark, perhaps even further information. And was it Daniel's imagination, or was there something accusing in his tone of voice?

'Didn't any—' Daniel cleared his throat—'Didn't anyone help the man? You'd have thought somebody . . . Well, I mean, in broad daylight.'

'Did it happen in the day?' Daniel felt that his face was turning crimson. He did not dare look at LeGrand's expressionless eyes. 'I suppose you might have heard about it. It must have been roughly the day when you arrived. But these attacks on Jews are really past a joke.' Surely the Doctor added that as a conciliatory gesture. Solomon Grimaud was the only person who was so paranoid as to mistake the Egyptian Nationalists' enemy. Daniel badly wanted to pay the bill and go . . .

The church clock struck the quarter hour. Standing in this mournful light, Daniel wished he could leave his hotel room too. If only the messenger would arrive he could step out and take the air. But it was now raining even harder. And noticing with a shock that the guns of the British ship were pointed towards the city, Daniel closed the window and walked over to the chaise-longue.

Feeling melancholy, he thought of his young wife. What would she be doing at this moment in their house in Lyons? Reading a book in the bright drawing-room? It overlooked yellow chrysanthemums and poplars. Or else embroidering parrots on tapestry circles and rectangles? They would eventually be set into fire-screens. It was he, Daniel, who gave Giselle ideas for her sewing. After all, he had once written verses and therefore had great

117

imagination. Nightingales, roses, ladies in crinolines—
these already stood before their hearths. The Benchimols
even had a footstool depicting a pair of artichokes.
(Giselle did not understand her husband's droll sense of
humour.)

Only once, when she asked Daniel, bent over his
accounts as usual: 'What shall I sew next?' did she refuse
his suggestion. For exhaling cigar smoke, and watching it
with bloodshot eyes, he said:

'The blue sky and sand.' But there was no design in the
desert . . .

Daniel was smiling to himself as he shifted his position
on the chaise-longue. How uncomfortable this hotel
furniture was! Remembering his home, he was impressed
by the strangeness of life. He would never have believed
it if someone had told him, while he was still a teacher in
Alexandria, that in four years time he would be returning
as a prosperous businessman, married and living in a
spacious house in the gastronomical centre of France.
Exquisite meals, despite LeGrand's warnings about his
liver; his initials worked in white silk on the corners of
pillow-cases and sheets; a solarium filled with orchids:
these were far removed from the damp room in Mex,
where Daniel had once eaten olives and saucisson sand-
wiches. How had he ever been able to write under those
conditions? On summer evenings he had been forced into
the streets by the overpowering stench of drains.

'And now tell me,' the Doctor had gone on to ask at tea
yesterday, 'to come to the most important question, are
you still writing?' He spoke in an even tone which almost
passed for sympathetic concern. And Daniel, being anxious
to relieve the tension of their recent remarks, was glad to
think it friendly.

'Yes, I'm writing,' Daniel answered, lying.

'Good.' LeGrand was looking at a plateful of éclairs as
if he expected to find his next remark in their midst. 'Had
anything published?'

'Not yet.' Daniel grew silent. He was recalling the
results of those years he had spent isolated from his

family, living as a teacher. They were contained in a hundred loosely written pieces of paper. He had used the backs of concert programmes and scribbled on the reverse sides of school registers. The ink was now faded, like that in old diaries. The pages were held together with a rusty paper clip. They were filed beneath his wife's cookery books in the bottom drawer of a roll-top desk.

Once, when Daniel had returned home unexpectedly in the middle of the afternoon, unfit for work after a drawn-out lunch with a client, he found Giselle sitting on the floor, the roll-top down, the drawer out, and her skirts covered in his manuscripts.

'What do you think you're doing?' he demanded. Giselle blushed. It was the first time Daniel had ever spoken harshly to his wife. A page trembled from her hand down onto the carpet.

'I was looking for a recipe,' she almost whispered.

Thereafter the desk was kept locked. He would not have his privacy invaded! But sometimes, walking alone in the garden before retiring, he realized that no matter how suitable his parents-in-law might have considered his family, Giselle's reason for choosing him had not been social or financial. For among her suitors, he had then seemed the least conventional. He once heard her boasting to her friends, just as the gentlemen appeared at the drawing-room door to rejoin the ladies after dinner:

'Well, my husband's not really a businessman. He's more of a writer.' She could as well have said an actor; the others were not easy to impress.

On his nocturnal strolls round the garden, Daniel often stopped by the tobacco plants. The spicy odour of their white flowers would remind him of the clove and incense which seemed to ride on sea breezes in Alexandria. They combined with the smells of mud and manure, quite different from the heady fragrance of this Lyons grass.

Surely life had been more concentrated, more intense, when he had been living in Egypt. In the bright light, on the flat land, everything seemed crystalline and defined. But Daniel tore a clump of tobacco flowers from the plants and threw it to the ground. He was just growing sentimental and poetic!

Alexandria had been no more than part of a long adolescence. Everyone wrote or, worse, grew religious at some time or other. For most it had already happened by the time they had left school. Falling in love with unattainable ladies, visits to backstreets housing women less ladylike than these, conversations in cafés with people who did not listen about drama and destiny; all these activities possessed a depressingly familiar ring. It had not been art, still less Alexandria, but a form of arrested development which invested those years with excitement and a sense of significance. And if Lyons or business ever felt stultifying and tedious, then it was natural that the growth of maturity might seem strange to one who had prolonged his youth.

Daniel lifted his fingers to his nostrils. The flower's scent remained . . . There had been orange blossoms in orchards, whose perfume pervaded the pavements. In the evenings the stars shimmered and leapt like dolphins. One saw them in schools travelling the wide spaces. The pyramids were on a vast scale.

Yet didn't he remember how impoverished his life had ultimately seemed? The school with its petty minded masters, jealous of anybody else's enthusiasms and achievements, proved intolerable by the end. Not that he had published anything worth mentioning: a five-line poem, which he paid to have included in a privately printed anthology, was not a proud boast.

Of course, he had made a mistake from the beginning. He should never have announced his intention of becoming a writer.

'When are you going to get something published?' the Head of his department asked, when Daniel declined to take an extra class after school on the grounds that he was writing.

'I've a short story coming out soon.' Naturally it was not really a lie. He was sure that his story *would* be accepted.

It had not been.

By now the fragrance had deserted his fingers. The white flower lay limp before him . . . How had he been able to bear the thought that he would never be successful as a writer? For he had tried; he had written, rewritten, and planned. How could the publishers dislike his poems or novelette? (One letter suggested that he become a literary critic instead.) He had almost forfeited his family and fortune. He had not known how he could stand to forfeit all hope as well.

Daniel left the garden. All lights, except for the hall lamp, were extinguished. Giselle had doubtless already fallen asleep. He might pause for a moment before penetrating the static air hanging about the great sweep of the wrought iron staircase like darkness. He reflected that he no longer entertained literary hopes. How presumptuous he had once been to imagine that his work was superior to the products of innumerable garrets and basements. There had been nothing unique in his life or the way he had lived it. The disinherited artist, starving while he created: there were many such heroes. They were clichés of the age. How ridiculous he seemed. He had taken himself so seriously. Such high ideals and intransigently held opinions!

'Your eyes are rather frightening,' a master's daughter once told him when he took her hand after a concert. 'I'm afraid that you may be, well, rather serious.'

To his right, as he ascended the stairs to his bedroom, Daniel saw the same eyes staring out of the darkness. Yet the pouches beneath them, the double-chin, and the anaemic flesh all seemed to dissolve in the mirror's shadowy grey. What if it were true? A kind of elixir, a magic mirror with the power to make people young.

Daniel shuddered. Such desires were idle. Now that he had learnt to live without longing and hoping, now that he trained himself to look no further backwards or forwards than an hour or a day, was he going to disrupt his routine and tranquillity by entertaining such thoughts? What was over, was over. Youth had passed, the moment had fled. Daniel climbed further into the darkness; it had obliterated his shoulder and face . . .

Tap. Tap. Tap.

Daniel was roused from his brooding. The hotel room was almost drained of light. As he moved from the chaise-longue to the window he realized that it had stopped raining. There was only the tapping of water falling from the roof onto his veranda. And a pale sun, like congealed red liquid, shed its last rays into the sea.

Benchimol was alarmed by his morbidity. Lately he had been too preoccupied with his feelings. Excessive introspection somehow made Daniel suspect that the life had flowed out of him. Yet the power and animal vitality which he felt he had lost, and yearned for, were merely mirages; they only seemed to have been real from this distance of time. Besides, did one have to believe oneself unique, or supremely potent, to feel alive?

Probably Daniel's mood reflected changes in his physiology. For in re-adapting to Alexandrian food and water he may have damaged his delicate liver; it was an organ whose malfunction could bring on depression, he well knew.

While Daniel stood by the window considering the possibility, he noticed his own image reproduced in scarlet again and again. It looked as if it had been painted on the watery rooftops round about him. He turned away. He was beginning to loom too large in his own thoughts.

Nevertheless, Benchimol could not help wondering which was worse: to long, like every other discontented soul, for a degree of recognition and grandeur of spirit which he knew he would never achieve; or to strike the pose, doubtless only half realizing it, of a failed writer living the rest of his anguished life without hope? Either way he would wake up each day angry and empty, savaged by the wild dogs of self-pity—no! It would require too great an abnegation of dignity.

Who was he, after all? A married man, successful and handsome, forthright and distinguished so he was often told. He had travelled, probably more than most of his contemporaries. He had seen life, or a substantial portion of it at least. Benchimol was certainly no Emperor whose indomitable ambition had forced him to seek victory even in that continent of memories and dreams to which he had been driven by defeat.

Tap.

The dripping had almost stopped. Only an occasional raindrop, releasing its tenuous hold on the window, finally slipped from the glass and yielded itself to the puddles below. There, on the streets prostrating themselves on straw mats away from the sun, the Arabs of Alexandria added their prayers to the high sounds of the muezzin who called the faithful to praise the one God.

'Like flies,' Benchimol muttered to himself. One more or one less, what did it matter? You just had to go into the streets, bursting with people, or down to the market, putrid with the indistinguishable smells of humans and carcasses, and ask if anyone was unique.

Even at Chatby and thousands of cemeteries like it, some long since covered by earth, it was impossible to tell which were the graves of emperors and heroes. And who could say when the doers of deeds, at the time immortal, had been offered up to the incomparable anonymity of sand?

Daniel had often seen processions making their way over to Chatby. He had even taken part in funerals like Mme Grimaud's. Yet looking from his window at the identical fez-covered heads below him, he wondered if the coffins could not equally well have contained one body as another. The mourners, whether dressed in black coats or *gallabiyas*, seemed, as they passed through his mind in an unbroken line, to participate in the burial of an unknown person.

On and on the crowds milled in the endless streets of the city. Each voice was absorbed by the general drone which deprived it of distance and depth. And continuing its progress, without faces or traces of identity, the procession wound on in Daniel's imagination.

Without explanations, neither reasons for departure nor

intimating their destination, they moved, interchangeable mourners in a march as inescapable as time. Daniel was aware of the repetitiveness: the funeral was almost like the passage of history. It seemed unimportant at which point one observed it, except that one saw more clearly if one's sights were trained on the part which had already gone by.

As he stepped onto the veranda, Daniel noticed the perspective with which he could see the crowd coiling through the streets round the hotel. But feeling tired, and momentarily closing his eyes, he found that he could no longer watch the inner procession with equal detachment. Nor could he banish it from his thoughts. It advanced, about to overtake and absorb him.

Daniel turned away, drawing the french windows behind him, and pulled the service cord. He pulled it again and again. Soon the boy who lighted the lamps reached M. Benchimol's room. He had travelled in the iron lift which moved with the grace of an invalid's chair. Daniel was waiting on the hall carpet, his door wide open.

'So there you are—at last!'

Daniel pulled his shirt cuffs below the sleeves of the frock-coat; he adjusted his cravat, and looked in the mirror as the young porter refilled the lamps with spirit. He watched impatiently as the boy trimmed the wicks, lit them with more than one match, and replaced the glass funnels. Daniel reached in his pocket for a coin, but the lamp in the bedroom had still to be lit. The bed cover and sheet were turned over; the windows and curtains adjusted; two pairs of shoes were taken to be cleaned.

The boy examined the tip he was given on leaving, forgetting to close the door in amazement at M. Benchimol's lavishness. Daniel, who almost slammed it with relief, asked himself:

'How many people could afford to be as generous as that?'

The sitting-room was now glowing with rich light. The angular, mahogany furniture appeared less obtrusive; even the chaise-longue looked almost elegant. Daniel noticed, for the first time, that it was covered with the same fabric as the curtains were made of. The few noises which penetrated the maroon drapes seemed insubstantial. Soon he was aware of no sounds at all. For a moment, imagining himself looking at the firedogs in his drawing-room in Lyons, he forgot his impatience with the messenger who was supposed to deliver a note. Surely that was a motif of artichokes woven into the floor rug. Then blinking, he wondered if Islamic art eschewed vegetable, as well as physical, representation.

Was there not something to be said for the sense of security which Daniel enjoyed through his money? His material comfort, constant though never ostentatious, marked him out as a conspicuous success. It was not that his achievement was a natural consequence of rejoining his father's already flourishing business. Daniel had shown flair and imagination of his own.

Daniel could not understand why he had just felt so depressed and discouraged. These days he was often nagged by irrational doubts about his own importance. The more he pondered, the more small things assumed exaggerated proportions.

He had also been anxious, he remembered, when he had first married. He might have been lying in bed with Giselle, exhausted but unable to rest. Fearing to move lest he wake his wife, yet wishing to make himself more comfortable as he used to in the days when he slept alone, he felt trapped by the dark canopy of their double bed. The whole house seemed heavy and stifling. He sweated and started coughing, counting the hours that must pass before morning. And Giselle's face, remote, locked in dreams he would never share, appeared callous and bland. For all the delicacy of her feminine ways, he seemed to glimpse the indifference of the blankly insensitive.

Had he perhaps made a mistake in his choice of a wife? There had been other women whom he could have married. Might he not have found a profounder partner, someone who was capable of understanding him better? Of course they had never been in love: perhaps it had been the problem. He had hoped that their good natured affection, born of domestic convenience, would eventually give way to more passionate feelings. But Giselle, far from calling him to the warmth of her arms from the routine of his office, simply reminded him of his unsatisfied desire, and the lack of issue from their otherwise conventionally successful marriage.

Who had failed? They did not know, and it was hardly a subject for conversation. Only in bed and on solitary walks round the garden, when Daniel's mind tended to turn to such things, did he imagine that it was he. Then he would consider himself a failure.

'Hard work. That's what they need. Hard work. And then they'll achieve something. I know their life's hell,' Daniel had said of the Arabs to LeGrand, later in yesterday's tea time conversation. 'But it's hell for all of us. Look at me.' He shrugged his shoulders and extended the palms of his hands in imitation of a gesture of modesty. 'Anything I've done has been the result of determination and will-power. Not that I'm saying it's much. But it's something.' He looked at the Doctor. 'Yes. It's something. A man needs to have built—well it doesn't matter what. But he needs to have built something. It's a matter of self-respect.'

Lying back now on the chaise-longue, looking down at the rug—the pattern really *did* remind one of artichokes—Daniel remembered that LeGrand had not answered for some time. He was watching the water tumbling down from the hotel fountain. It appeared to Daniel that the Doctor was studying the falling away of his own life. Then almost whispering, and not without a trace of bitterness, LeGrand remarked:

'Your ideas sometimes remind me of the things which Grimaud used to say.'

Thereafter they sat in silence. They had apparently exhausted every subject of mutual interest. Yet neither moved, for it was as if a vital energy, known to both, continued beneath their extinct conversation.

'I'm hoping to see Grimaud while I'm here,' Benchimol

said at last. 'It's the main—' he cast a fugitive glance at LeGrand 'or at least one of the reasons for my visit.' The Doctor was still watching the moon fleck the water with its unreal light as he answered:

'I should send him a message first if I were you. He doesn't see many people these days. You might find him in many ways a changed man.'

Benchimol later acted on the Doctor's advice. One of the bell-boys took his note, containing greetings and a dinner invitation, over to Ramleh. (Daniel had also hinted at his reason for wishing to see M. Grimaud.) Yesterday's answer, he remembered as he stood up—the chaise-longue, far from relaxing him, had given him a crick in his back— had been more cordial than he had expected. For although M. Grimaud declined the invitation on the grounds that he rarely ventured out, he hoped to ask Benchimol to an alternative function. And so, passing the gold pendulum of a grandfather clock as he paced back and forth, Daniel now found himself waiting for a second letter. He had been promised it by the late afternoon, but dusk was already fading into evening.

It was simply a question of manners Daniel told himself, growing even more impatient. Surely nobody needed a whole day and night to issue a summons to dinner. Moreover if one knew that somebody wished to make one a business proposition it was deplorable behaviour to keep him waiting, or so it would be considered in a civilized country. Of course, in a provincial backwater where Europeans treated each other as if they were Arabs, bargains were doubtless struck on the synagogue steps. But in Lyons and similar cities throughout France, Italy, and Germany, Jewish families like Daniel's had become established, and even indispensable, through commercial practices far removed from those of the soul.

Benchimol felt sure that self-interest alone should have prompted Grimaud to attend to a potential buyer of his fleet of cotton ships. Naturally the silence might indicate a sly business manœuvre, but it seemed out of character. He whom the Doctor had described as 'a changed man' would hardly indulge in obvious trickery. But then, what was 'in' and 'out' of character? Leopards were hardly renowned for changing their spots . . .

'I must say, you take a rather sour view of human nature,' Benchimol remembered LeGrand observing with unnatural coldness. (Further to the Doctor's remark about M. Grimaud, Daniel had wondered if it was really possible for anyone to alter.) LeGrand added, by way of a post-script: 'In fact, if you want to know the truth, I think that the most changed individual I've ever known is sitting, playing with his cigar-cutter, in the chair next to me.'

It was true, Benchimol remembered feeling, that various sad tendencies had coincided in the last four or five years of his life. Literary disappointments, fatigue with an impoverished existence, a sense of never having fulfilled his high hopes—all these had combined with his father's stroke. They made it impossible for Daniel, the eldest son, to maintain his indifference to the business. Perhaps he also wanted security, someone to live with, to love him. And what could have been easier than to return to his family and marry? Yet for all the dullness of spirit to which these events and decisions sometimes seemed to have led him, Daniel imagined the changes in his per-sonality to be improvements effected by maturity and experience. LeGrand, who had done nothing in his life, doubtless made his remark out of spite for Daniel's wealth and achievements. The matter was not worth discussing.

'How have I altered?'

The Doctor said nothing. But filling his corpulent body with air, he looked at Daniel and answered with his eyes while exhaling. LeGrand sank far back into the silk-covered chair, deflated, the life having passed out of him.

Now that had been grossly unfair, Benchimol reflected as he continued pacing in his hotel sitting-room. It was not he, but the Doctor, who had changed; LeGrand's every statement was jaundiced. Besides, if Daniel were not still energetic and alert he would hardly have travelled from Lyons to Alexandria, half the way over France and across the Mediterranean, in winter. And walking from window to wall, he recalled that all his 'faculties were intact'. (His mother often used the expression, common as he considered it, of her irritable husband whom she pushed round the frozen lily pond in his wheel-chair.)

Benchimol knew that he was emotionally alive. It was more than could be said of most other businessmen of his acquaintance. Which of them would have had the humanity to offer to run a firm for its invalid owner? (LeGrand had suggested that Daniel might go into partnership with M. Grimaud; his patient had still been frail on leaving the sanatorium four years ago.) And now that Benchimol was contemplating setting up international markets for his commodities—cheeses—was it not to Solomon Grimaud that he naturally turned for transport?

Daniel hoped that Grimaud would part with the ships. He had heard that he wished to consolidate and scarcely knew what he was doing. Surely Grimaud must realize that somebody did not offer to buy a fleet every day. It would be just too ungrateful of the old man to refuse to sell or to hold out for a favourable price. But then, when Daniel had last met him, shortly after the house in Ramleh had been re-opened, he had seemed strange: by now he might be even more unpredictable.

Grimaud had been sitting in what used to be his study. (It seemed much more than four years ago: Benchimol had not yet decided to leave Alexandria, still less to marry.) Daniel was surprised to find the room almost empty. Wooden lions' claws and golden eagles' heads still protruded through dust covers, but most of the furniture was standing, shrouded, in the hall. Even the bust of Napoleon—Daniel's every instinct told him that it *was* Napoleon staring beneath the sheet—was exiled from the study. A few remaining pictures and ornaments related to the Sahara. There was a series of water-colours of desert victories. Gunmetal models of pyramids stood on the floor.

'Come in,' Grimaud said, as Benchimol entered. He did not rise from the sofa. Shaking Grimaud's left hand,

Daniel noticed that the other arm was paralysed. It hung like a foreign body in his lap.

'I believe you're a writer.' Grimaud was smiling expectantly.

'Well, not so much any more.'

'It may surprise you, but I once thought about becoming one. Needless to say, it didn't materialize. I keep a diary now. It's all up here.' He tapped a temple knowingly. 'You're lucky that you're a writer. Always do what you really want to. It takes courage, but it's the only way to live.'

As Solomon Grimaud continued speaking on that October afternoon four years ago, Benchimol was convinced that the old man was either exceptionally wise or stupid. Rather than talking about the partnership, which LeGrand was sure was in the offing, Grimaud preferred to discuss Benchimol's recent past. It was a period which Daniel wished to forget.

Did the old man seek to unnerve Daniel? Perhaps he hoped that anxiety would render him more amenable to an unfavourable business proposition. Or did the meandering conversation herald, as seemed more likely, premature senility? If the former was so, Grimaud would certainly not have ended the interview just as Daniel reminded him of the reason for his visit:

'Ah! Yes. Naturally that will require some consideration. We must both think about it between now and next time.'

'The old fox!' Benchimol thought, passing the grandfather clock. Grimaud was not playing that same waiting game. 'Where the hell's his message?' Daniel heard himself asking.

At least Grimaud had not possessed the power to confine Daniel to a hotel room in those earlier days. (Benchimol supposed that he *could* leave his suite, though it would be better to be certain of receiving the note.) Soon after his interview with Grimaud, he remembered, his mother had sent him a telegram—tersely worded, but ending: 'with love'—which had contained news of his father's stroke. Daniel had immediately gone over to Ramleh to decline Grimaud's offer—had he ever made it? —of partnership.

The furniture was still stored in the hall. Only the bust, shrouded as before, had been moved upstairs. It stood by a bedroom from which a fourteen-year-old boy emerged. (Albert must be about eighteen by now, Daniel calculated, laying back again on the chaise-longue.) Benchimol noticed his first down, unshaved on the upper lip; there was a boil to one side of his mouth. The youth observed the visitor with dark unmoving eyes. He did not even look away when Daniel turned, embarrassed, to the study.

Benchimol felt he was being watched throughout his talk with Grimaud. (As a matter of fact, the old man showed more sympathy for his doubts about going into the family business than he would have suspected.

'Goodbye my boy.' He even rose, with difficulty, from the sofa.) Walking back, Daniel had imagined those eyes— penetrating, cold—still focusing on his back . . .

Knock. Knock. Knock.

Daniel sprang up from the couch. The bell-boy had arrived with a note.

Chapter 2

There had been no rain for two days. Mud had dried into strange shapes; the beaches looked as though they had just been formed; the sand was washed clear and glinted like crystal. Only a few clouds remained from the bad weather—clouds and the high winds that raced them along.

Daniel Benchimol felt the sun penetrate his thinning hair as the cab deposited him at Ramleh. Pressing a handkerchief to the small, but widening, patch of visible scalp where even the droplets of sweat were impregnated with the smell of eau-de-Portugal, he opened the gates. And taking out his watch, he smiled with satisfaction at finding that he was exactly on time: precisely ten o'clock.

M. Grimaud's letter had suggested that Daniel should meet him and his son at this hour. They would travel onto a sand yachting regatta together. M. Grimaud wondered if Daniel had ever seen the event. This year Albert would be competing. And they could be sure that the rain would have stopped in a couple of days. In this country bad weather was short-lived, if intense while it lasted.

As Benchimol walked up the steps to the house he noticed M. Grimaud sitting in an overcoat by the study window. He smiled but could not tell if the old man had returned the greeting: his face was almost lost in a grey beard and the shadow cast by the brim of a top-hat.

Benchimol was about to pull the bell when the front door swung open. He stood to one side as a young man aged about eighteen, wearing a white suit, gave a perfunctory nod and passed on. Daniel's way was further barred by servants carrying hampers, silver salvers, tureens, and travelling rugs. They were joined by maids bringing trays of breads and pastries from a side door. The elaborate lunch was tipped, willy-nilly, into a carriage.

The horse, sleek and well groomed, reacted against such unceremonious behaviour. It whinnied and neighed, jolting the crockery. Daniel saw the young man order the servants away with the back of a hand. Catching the bridle, Albert talked to the animal in a deep, smooth voice, while stroking its nose.

As the horse grew calmer, Albert became aware that the visitor had entered the house and stood watching him from the porch. The youth drew a pair of pince-nez from his top pocket and set them on the smooth bridge of his nose. The instrument of this affected maturity, Daniel thought to himself, jarred with the solemn adolescent eyes which it magnified. Then flushing as he returned the stare, Albert ran up the steps, two at a time.

'Benchimol? I'm Grimaud.' Daniel accepted the youth's

tacit, if brusque apology for his lack of hospitality b̲
extending a hand.

Daniel was escorted to the study. Albert did not enter.
He preferred to supervise the noisy passage of ice buckets
and champagne bottles through the house. Daniel noticed
through the open door that furniture was no longer stored
in the hall; but since the room in which he stood was
scarcely fuller than it had been four years ago, he assumed
that the ornaments and chairs had been redistributed.
Possibly Albert had appropriated them.

The noises of crates being dragged, and servants telling
each other what to do, continually interrupted Benchimol's
guttering conversation with M. Grimaud. (Daniel had
reminded himself on entering to offer his left hand. Why,
then, had he put out his right?) When what sounded like
an entire canteen of cutlery clattered to the kitchen floor,
Benchimol went over to the study door.

'I hope you won't mind if I close this,' he said to Albert
who was pausing outside the room.

'Not at all.' Albert had glanced inside; there was only
a battered sofa, a few old chairs, and his father.

'And how have you been?' Daniel asked Grimaud.
(Thank God! The noise appeared to have stopped.)

'Well.' Daniel felt sure that he had intended to say
something more. 'Well,' Grimaud blinked as a ray of
sunshine caught his eye. He suffered it for a little before
lifting his left hand, so fragile that Daniel imagined it
would atrophy as well, in a vain attempt to fight off the
intangible tormentor.

'Just like a baby!' Daniel thought to himself. There was
something almost endearing about the old man. How
could one entirely dislike him?

'It must be wonderful to live in such a beautiful house,'
Benchimol went on. He was looking round at the bare
walls.

'Yes, but rather lonely.' Even the water-colours had
been removed. 'My wife died rather young. You're
lucky—'

'At least you have your son.' Daniel, suddenly irritated,

wished that Albert would move away from the vicinity of the study; he was now giving orders to the grooms. 'He must be a big comfort.'

'Yes, Daniel'—it was the first time Grimaud had called him by his given name—'at least I have my son.' The old man repeated the words in a more tentative tone. As he watched the boy through the window, he seemed to be wondering if their meaning corresponded to any reality.

Soon all the preparations had been completed. Daniel helped M. Grimaud down the front steps.

'Now let's be careful. This marble's like glass.' Albert who had already installed himself in the carriage, observed his father's companion through quivering pince-nez.

'Leave him. I can manage.' The boy climbed down and offered his arm.

Chapter 3

All the way across the flat, hard-packed desert, white sails seemed to move without motion. They screened off shifting triangles of sky. And inside the members' enclosure, where Albert was being congratulated on winning a primary race, competitors adjusted the flapping sails of their craft. A few raised their goggles to examine a mast or a rudder; others holding walking-sticks gave seasoned advice.

'I say, Albert, you went like the wind,' said a boy of thirteen, imitating the supposed movement of the ship with his boater.

'But I thought you took that bend rather fast.' The speaker, himself disqualified in a previous heat, was no older than Albert. 'Of course, bends are a matter of . . .' he passed a hand through the air, searching for the right word, 'of experience.' He puffed at his cigar, burning the tip of his tongue on the smoke, as he wrapped a thumb and forefinger around the gold band.

The young man started, hearing an explosion. 'My goodness! What was that?' A number of ladies, their trembling hats as wide as the hems of their dresses, were promptly offered the contents of small bottles on handkerchiefs. And some, perhaps not realizing that they had merely heard the starter's pistol, resorted to the support of gentlemen's arms. Only Arabs, applying oil to the castors of yachts which had not yet competed, ignored the disturbance from their positions on the ground. And the noise, reverberating among the Europeans of Alexandria, was carried off into the wide folds of the desert by the same winds that scattered their ships on the sand.

'Congratulations,' a girl said almost privately to Albert, before anyone else had quite recovered. Her glistening black hair tumbled in rolls from the sides of a white hat; it fell over her lace covered shoulders. Albert gave a solemn, if awkward, bow. He took the fingers, dark through the crocheted gloves, and kissed them. Ignoring the giggles of the small boy, who had by now turned from one sensation to another, he omitted to release them.

'Would you like to join my party for champagne?' She answered with a shy smile.

Escorting the young lady to the pavilion—Albert felt sure that her sixteen years qualified her as a 'young lady'; besides, girls always looked older than they really were—he found that he could only overcome the feeling of being observed beneath innumerable parasols, and top hats, by preserving a dignified expression. Furthermore, since he did not wish to present his beautiful companion to friends or acquaintances, he hoped that his tongue-tied remarks would be interpreted as deep conversation; and that not wishing to interrupt a discussion of obvious importance, individuals who might normally expect a:

'Good morning', would be satisfied with a raised boater, and a slight nod. As it happened Albert's ruminations on etiquette proved unnecessary; they walked through the crowd unhailed.

On approaching the pavilion, Albert saw a man in his

mid-thirties standing on the veranda. He had a broad fore-head and thinning hair; he wore spectacles and stroked an incipient paunch, while gazing idly into the distance. Benchimol must have been there for the whole hour that had elapsed since their arrival.

Albert did not understand why his father had invited such a boring person to the regatta. It was unfair of him to expect his son to entertain a mere business client when he was competing for an important race. It was not only Benchimol's profession which Albert found antipathetic. The man's manner was disagreeable. His conversation seemed dissembling. There was a lack of candour in his evasive, watery eyes.

Benchimol's servility was especially conspicuous. Albert had noticed his readiness to take his father by the arm, to remind him to bring his cigar-case, to follow after him with his stick. He was continually trying to cover Grimaud's legs with a travelling rug, although the Doctor had told Albert that his father had never been better.

Had it been necessary to stop the carriage on the Boulevard Ramleh? The coachman was ordered to dis-mount and raise the hood. Although Benchimol looked at him reproachfully, Albert was right to insist that his father should simply lift his fur collar. The breeze had not been unpleasant, and M. Grimaud was certainly no invalid.

'Well done, Albert!' Benchimol called down from the pavilion. The boy noticed his father sitting in a deck-chair next to his client, his legs covered by a blanket—doubtless more of Benchimol's handiwork! 'Why don't you and the young lady join us for some champagne?' Benchimol smiled benignly.

'We will.'

Now that was another thing which Albert disliked in the man, his patronizing good-humour. Although he would not have cared a fig for Albert had he not been the son of a person with whom he presumably hoped to do business, he acted as if they had always been friends.

'I wonder if Albert remembers the time when we all

went to that splendid concert at San Stefano,' he had said to M. Grimaud, though for his son's benefit, as the carriage had left the outskirts of the city.

'I'm not sure,' Albert answered. 'I've been to San Stefano innumerable times.'

Albert might have relished his repartee a little more, strolling into the pavilion arm-in-arm with Catherine, 'the young lady', had he not been nagged at by the knowledge that his father was sitting above, exposed to Benchimol's influence. It probably never occurred to the old man that his client might be hoping to exploit him; possibly he never suspected that Benchimol's kindliness was sham. Albert would have joined them on the balcony at once if he had not been escorting Catherine.

Albert and Catherine found deck-chairs without difficulty. They sat by a marble-topped table, well back from the open windows. Long rays of winter light, traversing the raffia carpet and pine walls, fell short of their shoes. From the near-darkness the brilliant sails appeared to travel and turn as in dreams. All was quiet except for two ladies, unmoved by the races, dismembering the reputation of a lady from Cairo.

Still irked by the thought of Benchimol's proximity, Albert despaired of his father's judgment of character. How had he carried on business for all these years, especially among Arabs, without growing inured to professional charm? But then his father did not assess personality according to rational standards. He welcomed anybody who was a patient listener; he craved company and sympathetic attention.

Albert sensed that Benchimol might become a regular visitor to their house. Certainly his father would encourage him to call every day. For the old man, usually sitting alone in the study where it was impossible to say whether he read, slept, or just brooded, would beckon anyone passing his open door. He had even taken to chatting with the maids.

There were occasions too when Grimaud spoke to Albert: his son was usually leaving or entering the house.

He might ask for the time, inquire what book he was carrying, or try to discuss the current dangers to Europeans. Albert grew to recognize and dread these means of drawing him into conversation.

'I can't now,' he replied when his father invited him to sit for five minutes over a cup of chocolate. Had he not promised to meet friends on the Boulevard? Or else he might be late for his rendezvous with Catherine. 'I'm sure you see,' the boy added, leaving the study door abruptly. He disliked the sudden way in which Grimaud's animation would turn to abstraction.

'I understand,' the old man said. The windows returned his glazed stare.

Once Albert suggested to his father that he should go into the office. The old man had simply convinced himself that he was an invalid by sitting in this bare, unwelcoming room. Yet he seemed to have lost all will or ambition. His heart had gone out of:

GRIMAUD.

Confining himself daily to a few feet of Ramleh, seeing no further than his pillars and gates, he was scarcely aware that his cotton ships sailed the world's oceans. Grimaud listened inattentively to his manager's weekly report . . .

'Can you see?' Albert was called out of his thoughts by Catherine's question. She had been looking at him each time she turned away from the race, which was often. She pretended to find the moving sails intensely interesting whenever he began to return her glance. Albert hoped that she had not thought him as reflective and moody as adults had sometimes done.

'Very well thank you.' He was always oddly formal in Catherine's presence. 'In a few moments we will have some champagne.'

Before them, expanses of white canvas scurried over the desert in the late morning sun. Ships faded into the distance. A brass band played a sad march.

'Would you like to borrow my opera glasses?' Catherine

asked, slipping her hand from the fingers with which Albert had just touched it. She offered him the small binoculars by their gold handle. Albert set the lenses firmly to his eyes, without thanking her. Lips pursed, he saw sails rise out of the sand.

'. . . from Marseilles to Casablanca and Tunis . . .' Albert could hear snatches of Benchimol's conversation with his father floating down from the balcony. '. . . cargoes . . . Alexandria . . . even the heart of black Africa . . .' There were craft so far distant that they floated beyond the range of the glasses. Like vapours, they unloosed at the horizon: Albert doubted that he had ever seen them at all.

The names of ports continued falling from the veranda. There were rivers and oceans, harbours and lakes. The desert seemed endless and blinding; it stretched beyond the plain where the yachts were sailing. Albert saw himself adrift in vast seas of sand, far from cities and people. He was lost, and would never be found, in the overwhelming wastes . . .

'What's it all for?' Albert remembered his father thinking aloud, as the carriage had drawn into the desert an hour and a half ago. Grimaud's eyes, dark beneath the brim of his top hat, appeared like illuminated sockets; they glistened on their way through the sand. 'What's the purpose of this waste? Nothing grows here. It's just sterile.'

'No purpose,' Benchimol answered. 'It's like life, just matter. The dunes are blown like this, or like that.' He indicated with the back of his hand. 'It's all without reason.' The wheels and the horse's hooves moved in rhythm, their sounds gathered up into the wind.

'No reason?' Albert's father had asked. 'You think it's simply wanton waste?'

'Just a waste,' Benchimol repeated. He did not look at the sand. 'Of course it can still support some forms of life: bedouins and camels, for example. But then do they ask more of the desert than to exist?' He continued, his voice strangely dulled: 'If we could simply be content to exist, instead of longing for the moon, we might be saved from arid lives . . . .' The sound died in his throat.

For a while the conversation lapsed. There were only the animal sounds of the driver urging on the horse. Ahead, on a mound, shattered and disused, stood a Napoleonic fort. Its two remaining walls, joining in a corner, were defined by the brilliant light.

'And you, Albert, what do you think? What do you suppose is the meaning of life?' Albert detested Benchimol's tone of voice. Its artificial brightness barely hid the man's indifference to the answer. His disingenuous smile proclaimed the approval he expected from M. Grimaud for having drawn his son, no matter how artlessly, into the conversation.

Albert recalled looking at the ruin through his pincenez before answering. He sought some statement, short of the barbaric, which would dispose of Benchimol's paltry philosophy.

'What the point of your life is, I couldn't say. But for myself, I believe it's possible to achieve one's aims if one only has the will.'

'But what about that?' Benchimol pointed to the crumbling walls. 'What's left of the man who successfully willed that? Even great achievements are short-lived, you know.'

'That is left,' Albert had answered. 'We're remembering him now, aren't we?' . . .

'. . . Samarkand . . . Timbuktoo . . .'

Albert was not certain if the names he had seemed to hear had been the words floating down from the pavilion balcony. Distracted from his memories, he noticed Catherine's face: the sides of her mouth were curved upwards.

'You can tell me what you're thinking about.'

'Oh! Nothing really.' He closed his eyes as she passed a hand over his furrowed brow.

'Samarkand . . .'

He seemed to see silk caravans sliding down dark falls of sand . . .

Catherine stopped stroking his forehead. As Albert opened his eyes he remembered something his father had said:

'I don't know, but it seems to me that the things which waste themselves, like the sea and sand, are by far the most beautiful.'

Chapter 4

M. Grimaud was sleeping on the balcony. While others deserted the pavilion, taking their children to see the magic-lantern show which had been set up in a marquee during the interval between lunch and the start of the afternoon's racing, he had covered his shoulders with a travelling rug and dozed off in a deck-chair. Daniel had offered to sit with him, talking in the winter sun, but Grimaud sent him off among the couples strolling beneath the red and yellow striped awnings of improvised cafés. Perhaps he would find Albert; they might discuss the boy's strategy for the final race.

It was not that Grimaud was bored with Benchimol— far from it. He found Daniel considerate and patient. But as one grew older it became more difficult to remain in the constant company of other people, no matter how much one liked them. No discourtesy was intended if after half a bottle of champagne, and several hours of business, he sought a certain solitude and repose.

Grimaud moved in his chair; the light, surprisingly bright for this time of year, was shining in his eyes. Below him yachts were at rest, their sails lowered, in the competitors' enclosure. Only a few craft continued exploring the sands.

'I'm afraid I've done most of the talking this morning,' Grimaud remembered Benchimol saying over lunch. Daniel raised a finger for the old man's glass to be re-filled. 'But then it's not every day that somebody offers to buy a whole fleet of ships.'

Albert was looking up expressionlessly at Benchimol's smiling face. He was sitting next to Catherine. An Arab servant dressed in a pair of cotton pantaloons, a jellak, and fez, set a couple of quail on her plate.

'I'm sure you'll agree I've made you a handsome offer. Naturally it'll require some consideration. You don't have to make up your mind immediately.'

Grimaud felt that Benchimol had altered over the last four or five years. He was more compliant, less abrasive. But hadn't everyone changed? While Daniel spoke of Grimaud's ships sailing the Mediterranean with his cheeses, there was his characteristic touch of vision. For even the Bantu, in his world of endless possibilities, might disdain human flesh when confronted with Camembert.

'Of course my company couldn't release the whole sum at once. We'd prefer to pay you in instalments over a period of time.'

Grimaud's mind wandered with the white fleet flecking the desert. It drifted over the great spaces . . .

'In the first two years we'd like to pay you with a proportion of the profits . . .'

Vessels floated over the horizon into seas where no ship had previously ventured.

'Our lawyers will draw up the contract . . .'

Now, also, half an hour later, remembering the mellifluous voice, he grew drowsy . . .

Grimaud woke shivering. The travelling rug lay in a heap by the deck-chair; he must have shaken it off during his sleep. Still feeling unreal for a moment, he took a lady standing by the pavilion for a nun. The scarlet feathers on her fantastic white hat bounced as a gentleman led her off to watch the first race of the afternoon.

And there in the distance, chasing his boater, was Albert. He ran, pulling Catherine along behind him. They giggled as she kept stopping to pull down her skirts with her free hand. Then Albert would draw her towards him, pretend to whisper in her ear, but kiss her. Grimaud fondled his beard, smiling at his son's mischievous behaviour.

A RACE

Grimaud remembered that he had first met his wife at about Albert's age. It had been at one of the extraordinary soirées which Ivette's Aunt Stella, newly returned from a stay in Paris, used to give. They were the kind of functions to which nothing short of blood-ties would make one return. Solomon and Ivette, eighteen and seventeen respectively, sat out on the lawn, preferring sherbets to the second half of a recital of Chopin's piano music rescored for the violin.

When the waiter, offering them wine, turned back to the house, they laughed at his tail-coat. Aunt Stella should not have dressed her servants in European clothes, especially ill-fitting ones, no matter what the staff wore in French hotels. Egyptians looked best in loose Arab garb.

Grimaud's attention was attracted once more by his son. Albert and his companion were posing for their photograph at one of the stalls which had sprung up around the marquee. The boy tucked his boater under one arm and took Catherine's hand with the other. The black cloth attached to the camera wriggled like a two-legged insect before them. Grimaud was surprised that the girl's skin, though tanned like all Europeans' who lived in the Middle East, was not darker. In her lace dress and hat one might never have known that her mother was half-Egyptian: she could have been Syrian or Greek.

Grimaud remembered how beautiful his own wife had looked on their wedding day. Recently he had been turning through the photographs: many were brown, though they still bore the roseate emulsion with which the photographer had tinted Ivette's cheeks. Looking back at that time, Grimaud could only think of tiered cakes and good advice. Most of his contemporaries had married.

He recalled the commotion caused by the engagement of Catherine's parents. The night before the wedding, the food having been prepared, the trousseau finished, and the invitations sent out long ago, her paternal grandmother became hysterical. The servants even considered sending for a doctor. She—an Italian Jewess who had married a

Count—would not allow an Egyptian to wed her son. She screamed it out in five languages, including Arabic.

The Countess wept through the service, drank too much champagne, and finally returned to her estranged Italian spouse. Years later Aunt Stella received a letter from her saying that her new husband, a Marquis from Malta, had been beating her like an Oriental despot. The envelope bore a Gozo postmark; the island was her sanctuary. Just before dying, the Marchioness had written again:

'My life has been so sad that I might as well have married for love, as my son did.'

Grimaud suddenly forgot the past as he noticed his son and Catherine smiling awkwardly for the photographer. (The old man was disturbed to find himself beaming inanely also.) Albert had brought the girl home, though she was hardly the first person whom he had invited to dinner. She was attractive and dull; but then Grimaud felt certain that other friendships with young ladies would intervene between the present and his son's marriage.

By now Albert had left Catherine to prepare himself for the race. Standing by the yacht in the competitors' enclosure, he ran a hand over the prow. And looking nonchalantly into the distance, he spoke to their coachman who was examining the hull in his new capacity as boatman.

Grimaud could read the yacht's name—'IVETTE'—from the pavilion balcony. The craft had been launched shortly before he had left the sanatorium. He asked the Mother Superior to perform the christening, although he was not a Catholic. And Professor Valence had shaken hands, almost speaking in a whisper, at the end of the desert ceremony.

Sometimes Grimaud wanted to thank the Mother Superior, but how and for what? He would realize that he knew her neither superficially nor intimately enough to express his gratitude in clichés. For although he had never discovered her nationality and name, he was sure that she almost understood what he had suffered.

There had been occasions in those years when he had

strayed into the chapel. It was cool and a change from his room. He sat for hours in the shadows, as he had after Ivette's death, feeling that time had started going backwards. It was returning, drawing him with it; he could not stop it; he lacked the strength to resist. He looked at his hands: they were familiar, but no more his than the face he had once kept seeing in a study mirror. The way his tongue rested in his mouth, the clothes that clung to his skin, his drawing of breath, they all seemed unnatural and unreal.

Gazing at the picture above the altar—Christ crucified, half the face obscured by dark hair and the head haloed with livid light—he suddenly knew that he was dead. He could still see: the Mother Superior, all in white, was sitting in the pew next to him, attentive to his silence. Yet he was really dead. He had never known such sorrow.

Later he began to feel that he was living; how long after he could not say. It was not life like other people's. He took on the existence of all he saw. Once in Professor Valence's house he was reduced to despair by a bowl of flowers. He was anguished by the knowledge that he alone must bear the burden of all suffering and beauty. If only he could pass the weight on . . .

'Don't leave me!' he shouted to Valence. The Professor, sitting with his habitually mute patient, had allowed his mind to drift for a moment towards problems of his own.

Grimaud remembered the day he had left the sanatorium. He felt both happy and sad. Riding out of the quiet buildings and gardens into the greater silence beyond, the eagerness with which he had anticipated his departure turned to acute trepidation. Would he be able to live without the sympathy he had grown used to? Might his feelings, now largely purged of distortions, prove unsuited to the outside world?

As the train moved through the desert, his past behaviour appeared like memories of somebody else. It almost seemed inconceivable that he should ever have been contorted or unkind. Why, when his wife had been ill, had he not simply expressed his panic and love for her?

Why had he grown increasingly brutal when Ivette's condition had declined? He really wanted to live in peace with her; for her he wished rest. Perhaps these impulses had been so corrupted by his fears and furies that she never recognized the inexpressible affection glimmering in his angry eyes. Perhaps she had died thinking he hated her . . . He put a hand to his face. It was too awful to think of. Never, never would he make the same mistakes with Albert.

Looking down at his son from the deck-chair, now that four years had passed, Grimaud repeated his promise. He would never impose his will on Albert. Recently he had spent all day in the study, showing no more than an unobtrusive interest in his life. Grimaud had concealed his hurt at the boy's reluctance to share his time, and though he suspected that Albert was somehow ashamed of him he always kept his temper.

Grimaud's attention was suddenly attracted by an argument at the entrance to the competitors' enclosure. Benchimol was trying to pass the old Arab at the gate without producing a bribe or an official card. For some reason Albert, who was standing within, made no attempt to help him. (He might have corroborated Benchimol's claim to belong to a member's party.) The boy just stood watching the fracas. And only when Benchimol had finally entered, virtually pushing the old Arab aside, did Albert walk towards him. He beckoned him over to the yacht.

Grimaud was saddened by his son's reaction to Daniel. Albert could sometimes seem to be devoid of good manners or charm. Indeed, in his least attractive moments Albert resembled Benchimol as he had been in his days as a schoolmaster. Of course, the boy had not only behaved coldly with Daniel. He was difficult with all his father's friends. Grimaud might have minded less if only acquaintances had been alienated; but these days he sustained closer relationships than he had sought as a married businessman.

If Albert had not scorned his company, Grimaud would have judged his son jealous of Benchimol's claims

146

on his time. The boy appeared no less envious of his father's friendship with the Doctor. Albert addressed Daniel and LeGrand with equal sarcasm and disdain; he overrode their opinions in an almost insulting manner.

Just as painful to Grimaud were his son's ungenerous remarks about others.

'He's just a frightened old woman,' Albert said recently, when his father suggested inviting the Doctor to dinner. Grimaud often recalled the boy's hackneyed words; though consoling himself with the thought that Albert would learn tolerance with age, he perhaps felt that their hearer had provided their true target.

Yachts began emerging from the enclosure. Grimaud saw Albert give Benchimol his jacket and boater before donning a long leather coat, a peaked cap, and gloves. And when his craft had been pushed to the starting line, the boy even produced a pair of goggles. Then sails, previously flapping and distended, were tautened. A hand, rising from a starched cuff, fired a pistol into the air. The sound boomed over the tops of silk hats, bonnets, boaters, and bald heads. Moments later it travelled back from the desert.

Chapter 5

The wind sent Albert sailing so fast that he barely had time to observe the spectators. Only when he leaned backwards, gripping the side as the yacht lurched on a turn, could he see the pavilion and marquee, upside down, across the intervening desert. Or else, just looking over his shoulder to make out how far the other competitors were behind, he caught an elongated glimpse of the crowd. A few bars of music reached his ears from the distance.

There was no time to think; only images passed before him. The wheels were like hooves, running wild and drawing him forward. And the sheet, filled by the breeze, would carry him into the sky.

At one point, when he almost collided with another yacht—ill-directed—Albert had hardly been able to see. Although the light was clear he could barely control the wheel. He was suffocating despite the limitless space. Presences, perhaps his own muscles, seemed to prevent him from steering. For some time after his hands were trembling and sweaty.

A little later—it could have been a minute or a moment —Albert realized that he had overtaken all the other yachts. He watched their sails fall behind. The space of sand between his stern and the next prow grew like his shadow. And anticipating victory, Albert almost heard the hero's welcome he would receive.

The band had begun playing the triumphal march from *Aida*. An Italian ice-cream vendor sang out the tune. His resonant voice lauded the return of the latterday barges until tears sprang to his eyes. They anointed the same cassata as he had sold on the steps of *La Scala* when Verdi's operas were being performed.

Albert glided over the finishing line at the head of the fleet. The sun caught the brass rim of a euphonium. It was reflected by the slides of trombones. In the blur he thought he saw a face; the mouth was composed in a smile. And waving her parasol, Catherine was surely calling his name.

Chapter 6

Benchimol turned to watch the finish. He had been ambling through the fair, where sturdy boys repeatedly failed to knock coconuts off their stands despite palpable hits. He passed gypsy caravans in which every young lady discovered that her fortune was identical with her friends'. It was impossible to see who was winning. Only the tip of a mast protruded above the dense crowd. Far beyond, in the desert, sailed the rest of the armada.

Daniel knew that if he had wanted to follow the races more carefully he should probably have procured the programme listing each competitor's name and yacht number. Yet he had hardly come here on pleasure—although the food, especially the saffron in the fish mousse, had been delicious. If he desired a better view he could always rejoin M. Grimaud on the pavilion balcony. But then it might be better not to bother the old man while he considered Daniel's proposition.

Wild cheers were now rising as the mast came to a standstill. Coloured streamers, orange blossoms and raspberries filled the air. One child was sucking a lemon directly before the band. The conductor, on an imploring look from the trumpeters, included the back of the boy's head in the path of his next baton stroke.

Naturally the only person whose result would have remotely interested Benchimol was Albert; he doubted that he would command the leading position. Daniel lit a cigar with his back to the breeze blowing down from the finish. The winner was still being applauded as Daniel sauntered away from the race.

Daniel was pleased with the way in which he had spoken to Grimaud this morning. He felt that he had appealed to the old man's best interests without bullying. If Grimaud were to relinquish the burden of directing the fleet— especially since he took no interest in it—he would not be the loser . . .

Daniel could hardly believe that it was Grimaud standing and cheering on the balcony. Who would have imagined that he would have the energy to throw his hat into the air?

Chapter 7

As workmen dismantled the marquee, the late afternoon sun strained through a skeleton of dark tent poles.

Booths which had once contained performing monkeys and bearded women, stood stripped to their bamboo frames. Only the skirts of departing ladies caught the wind for a moment. Programmes raced unhindered through the members' enclosure in which footsteps had already been eroded from the sand.

M. Grimaud watched the yachts, their sails lowered as if in bereavement, being pushed into the boathouse. Albert was directing the movement of his own craft. His father had given it to him in celebration of his victory.

'If only your mother could see you now.' (He had known the sentiment was clichéd.) The long mast was the last to enter the shelter. (Grimaud furtively wiped his eyes with the back of a hand.)

Opposite him in the carriage, where he was waiting for his son to finish, sat the young lady to whom Albert had offered a ride. Grimaud observed her while hampers of dirty plates were being loaded. There were still the smells of fish and garlic; silver dishes looked like gunmetal in the dying light.

Catherine was fingering the handle of her parasol, aware of M. Grimaud's scrutiny. Undoing and doing up the clasp of a cameo, she watched Albert recover his winner's cup from the lighted interior of the pavilion.

An hour before, when he had been presented first with his trophy and then his father's sand yacht, Albert had tried to leave the crowded club-room and join Catherine on the balcony. The boy was surprised by his desire to escape the admiring smiles and comments. Yet he had only had one wish, to absent himself from the suffocating atmosphere of congratulations. He had almost completed the gamut of handshakes and embraces when he was intercepted by a neighbour's wife. She was dressed in shantung silk printed with a tiger skin design.

'You must be very proud of your son.' She leant over and kissed Grimaud. 'And you, Albert, must feel very grateful for having such a wonderful father. But darling'— she had hugged him—'what is your present called?'

'CATHERINE.'

Catherine's observation of the pavilion was disturbed by Benchimol's entry in the carriage. He leaned back in his seat, lighting a cigar. The last rays of light were lost in the smoke which he exhaled.

'What a wonderful day it's been.' He turned to Grimaud for confirmation, but the old man had fallen silent. Daniel could not tell if his eyes were open or closed.

They were waiting for Albert. He appeared on the balcony for a few moments, his trophy dangling from his little finger. As the boy stood there, the fiery horizon faded into the darkness. Somewhere in the desert, the scene of his victory, he could hear the howling of a pariah-dog.

PART II
Two Years Later

Fasting and Feasting

Chapter 8

A cannon was mounted on the hills at Mex. It overlooked the mounds of limestone heaped up at the mouths of quarries. It pointed past the narrow tracks where Arabs loaded boulders into open carriages drawn by metal trains. (They worked so slowly—stripped to the waist, with white cloths bound around their frizzled hair—that their movements appeared like mere distortions of the sunlight.) The cannon, directed across mud huts so like each other that they blurred into a dusty haze, pointed beyond the dockyard. It would be fired into the sea at sunset.

There were more people in Alexandria this Ramadan than Dr. LeGrand had ever known before. He had always found it difficult to move through the Arab quarter, especially during the fast. For Egyptians, enfeebled during the day, would lounge in sunless streets and alleys. Or irritable and faint, they congregated in the precincts of closed cafés; some sat and talked at the empty tables. Arguing and telling stories, they awaited the boom of the cannon and the call to prayer. Even when drummers carried on the blast, the Arabs, having washed their hands and mouths and drunk bowls of milk and *harira*, passed into the avenues and squares. Carrying torches, they filled the city until dawn. Yet this year pilgrims, on their way from North Africa to Mecca, swelled the already crowded Arab quarter. They sought lodgings at private huts and inns.

The Doctor, putting a handkerchief to his nose, was passing a group of Negroes who shared a wooden shed with goats. They probably sat there fasting all day he thought, trying to walk a little faster. He wanted to arrive at his flat by lunchtime.

Others, whom LeGrand had thought might have been Tunisian from their delicate features, had installed themselves on the beach. The residents of Ramleh and Camp Caesar had instantly sensed the risk to European bathers. Their health and safety were in danger—and in the case of their wives and children who knew what else? The Doctor, himself, was asked for his support. Flattered, he agreed to sign a petition. Now these Arabs lay before him, turned from the edge of the Mediterranean to streets where they lived on prayer mats set down by the sides of open drains.

LeGrand passed on quickly. He rarely entered this quarter. Although it was autumn the noonday sun was still fierce. If he did venture this far it was generally for a professional reason. But usually, unlike this morning, the police requested his services. He had previously imagined that Egyptians had their own ways of dealing with disease, although he could scarcely imagine what they might be.

Besides it was surely too dangerous to wander through such narrow streets. The authorities had even thought of imposing a curfew.

'Sometimes things get better, but then they always get worse again,' the Doctor remembered saying to Benchimol. Although Daniel had started dividing his time between Lyons and Alexandria during the last two years, LeGrand seemed to see less of him. He was always arranging shipments for his fleet, meeting bankers and buyers, or entertaining his young wife in the evenings . . .

LeGrand felt certain that what he had said was true. He knew too many people who had been robbed or reviled to entertain much hope that the situation would improve.

Acquaintances had been attacked; patients' friends were injured for no reason. He recalled an Armenian lady, the grandmother of a boy whom he had treated for whooping cough: her glasses were broken in her face as she stooped to recover them from the ground, late one summer after-noon. And somebody—had it been Benchimol?—told him of a man who was murdered at the port in broad daylight. Of course, that was in the days when Daniel had found time to have tea with him . . .

These Arabs seemed quite insensitive to the suffering which they caused. Were they entirely ungrateful for all that had been done for them?

Earlier this morning, while the Doctor was examining someone's throat, a small boy, indistinguishable from the countless juvenile waiters delivering glasses of coffee in wrought iron frames to shop proprietors, had entered his surgery without knocking.

'What do you want?' LeGrand demanded roughly, annoyed that the maid had not stopped the urchin from interrupting what might have been the first of many con-sultations with a new patient. The boy did not answer in French, as most would, but urgently pulled at the Doctor's cuff. LeGrand freed his arm and pointed to the waiting room. (He smiled in embarrassed apology at the cor-pulent Greek standing with his braces down and collar off.) But the boy would not go. He started talking excitedly in what LeGrand thought was Turkish, attaching himself once more to the sleeve.

'Go away!' the Doctor commanded in Arabic. (The six languages he spoke stopped short of Turkish.) The Greek's mouth re-opened, though not for examination. 'Police!' LeGrand threatened. 'Police'. Yet the boy, undeterred, answered in execrable Arabic.

'Ill.' He rubbed his stomach and opened his mouth, pretending to gasp. 'Father. Ill.' And again he pulled at the cuff; only this time, instead of shouting, the Doctor tried to reassure his patient—and followed.

LeGrand soon realized just how far the boy expected to take him: the child pointed to the shantytown by the harbour. Then running, mistakenly imagining that the Doctor would do the same, he turned back and took the sleeve once more.

LeGrand was amazed that he had agreed to go at all.

He had felt danger as soon as the small messenger had started tugging at his cuff. By the time he had put on his hat he had felt certain that he was walking into a trap. Thereafter, LeGrand's fear had intensified with each step.

Why, he asked himself, measuring the weight of his bag in his right hand, should he have been chosen from all the doctors in Alexandria? Louvier was just as near the Arab quarter, or for that matter what about old Morin? LeGrand was sure that he had no enemies. Certainly he scolded the maid but most people treated their servants more harshly; besides, he had been telling her off for years. Perhaps she had let someone know what his flat contained: he lived so simply that there was nothing of which even an Arab would care to rob him. But then she had surely long since detected the Doctor's brusque good humour, and was naturally devoted to him.

The boy hurried him on. LeGrand was almost running through the glaring streets. It hurt his eyes to look at the buildings. Violence, he knew, could sometimes be excited without reason. He himself had seen the meaningless cruelty of which an inflamed mob was capable. (Could he escape down this side street without the messenger noticing? It was absurd that a grown man should be afraid of breaking loose from a mere boy.) The small hand continued to drag him forward by the sleeve.

As LeGrand entered the maze of dark streets, he felt so exhausted that he was barely able to distinguish the flies collecting about his face from the black spots he seemed to see gather before him. People crowded around; women were wailing through veils at narrow windows; and Arabs, cupping their hands, cried out to the sky.

He was pressed into a hut where the boy, having never released his cuff, had led him. There, shivering beneath a goat skin blanket, lay a middle-aged man. His fine white robe, well over six feet long, hung over the bed. Its hem, embroidered with gold thread, broke over the pillow; and coiled round the garment, with leather thongs tied to its end, was a whip decorated with blue, enamel beads.

The man sat up as the door opened. He blinked at the

slight light with wild, frightened eyes. LeGrand noticed the dried skin and veins on the backs of his hands. His broad shoulders were bony; hollows gaped in his wide, unshaven face.

He pointed to his mouth and whined imploringly: he was too weak to talk. But the people who entered the hut, filling it with the noise of their interminable wailing, refused to give him water. Not even his own son dared pass him the earthenware pitcher. Only when the cannon had been fired would this man, the powerful leader of an orthodox Turkish community in the Lebanon, so LeGrand learned afterwards, be lawfully permitted to moisten his cracked lips.

The Doctor half expected to be restrained as he bent down, filled a cupped hand, and offered it to the man to drink. Yet the moaning simply continued, while his fingers and palms were drained again and again. The small boy watched—it was impossible to see with what emotion —as his father turned on his side and groaned. He vomited a trickle of gruel-like mucus. It lay on the already slimy reed floor.

Once the examination had ended, LeGrand realized that the wailing had changed to cheers. He was patted on the back and given cigarettes. Children followed him, offering to carry his bag.

Only now as the Doctor neared the outskirts of the Arab quarter, going through the strange sequence of events in his mind, did the followers straggle and finally fall right behind. He looked back, resting alone for a moment. How could one ever retrace one's steps among all that rotting timber and mud?

LeGrand had tried to refuse payment for his glance at the wasting body. He doubted whether his pills would do more than stop the diarrhoea. (They were all that seemed even remotely appropriate in his medical case.) But the Turk, his fevered eyes momentarily ecstatic, pressed the coins on him; and outside the thanksgiving had already begun.

Yet what could LeGrand do for these people? He sighed,

still looking back at the squalid shelters. It was an impossible situation. The dark mass took his eyes down to the harbour and dock. There on the glistening water, white ships moved into the Mediterranean. He saw a flag quiver and suddenly crispen; its blue stripes stretched out before the limitless horizon and flapped beneath an even bluer sky.

So Benchimol had decided to keep Grimaud's colours. He had possessed that much sentiment for the old man at least. On almost any day one could see ships of his fleet picking their route through the British navy. LeGrand imagined Daniel watching them with satisfaction from a suite in the Cecil. Doubtless he never looked at the huts which intervened.

The Doctor turned back. It was nearly lunchtime. He began hurrying on.

There was the smell of fresh bread as he passed a Jewish bakery. He looked at the display of confectionery and seed rolls. He hoped that the maid had not forgotten to buy his cakes from the *pâtisserie* on Ramleh Square, now that their usual shop was closed all day. She became quite impossible during Ramadan.

The Doctor often wished that they would abolish the fast—or at least cheat a little more. He had occasionally left out a tempting peach or box of cheese in the kitchen. Why was it then that the maid, irritable and inefficient, chose this as the sole matter about which to be honest?

LeGrand swallowed as he remembered the cheese. He was feeling hungry. These days one could buy *Camembert*, *Munster*, *Caprice des Dieux*. He could almost see them running on the cheese-board . . .

He helped up the blind Arab whom he had bumped into while striding along . . .

Of course, Benchimol would never have spared a thought for these wretched people. (LeGrand remembered the Turk's face: the skin had been stretched like sail-cloth over the bone.) They could all starve as long as he satisfied his markets. And besides, did Daniel really imagine that before the advent of his business nobody had ever tasted good cheeses? They were not all provincials. The Doctor himself had studied in Paris.

Away in the distance the ships continued their imperceptible movement. It was impossible to tell whether they were coming or going. They hovered on the measureless line.

LeGrand knew that his disenchantment with Daniel was not just the result of a growing bitterness with life. His wit was tart, sarcastic even; he had seen things recently which would have made anybody take a caustic view of human nature. Yet he was really a compassionate man. After all, it was more for Benchimol's treatment of others than of himself that the Doctor grieved.

LeGrand felt the utmost sympathy for M. Grimaud. He had heard that Daniel had pressed the old man into selling his fleet at an absurdly low price. That much was common knowledge. But what was less well known at the dinner tables of Alexandria was the way in which Benchimol had succeeded in striking the bargain. The Doctor could imagine it. Daniel would have flattered, avowed good intentions, appealed to reason. He could seem eminently reasonable. How hollow it all sounded to one who had heard them arguing years ago! Worse still, Daniel had undoubtedly taken advantage of Grimaud's mental weakness. It was a premeditated plan. Benchimol would have seemed so concerned and devoted that in the end Grimaud might have done anything for him. He still treated him like his own son.

Now, two years after, the old man was almost abandoned. Daniel had only called at Ramleh once the last time he was in Alexandria—and that was with his wife. (She herself had not been invited.) Daniel brought Giselle to the restaurant when they invited the Doctor to dinner. Presumably they could eat like that every night . . .

LeGrand had sometimes considered going over to Ramleh himself. But since Daniel had grown so close to the old man, he was rarely invited; and he certainly did not feel that he could just visit on impulse. Would it not be rude to call one evening when he had nothing else to do?

As a matter of fact the Doctor and Grimaud were meeting tonight: it would be the first time in several months. LeGrand was somewhat surprised that the old man had accepted the Mother Superior's invitation to the All Souls' feast; but then he had altered since the days when he lectured people on Zionism.

Even so, it was doubtful whether Grimaud, previously punctilious, would have undergone such a drastic change as to receive persons unannounced. And the Doctor rarely found time to pay social calls. There was always his practice to keep him busy; while the possibility of violence made it wiser to stay at home. He would sit in the flat, smoking and thinking . . .

LeGrand felt certain that Benchimol would never contact him again. He might as well put such an ungrateful young man out of his mind . . .

Had Daniel forgotten LeGrand's inexplicable anger over dinner? The Doctor had accused him of forsaking his ideals. It was not a matter to speak of so violently before the man's wife. Naturally people were unpredictable: Daniel might have forgiven the incident. (LeGrand had never bothered to ask if the note of apology, which he had left at the Hotel desk, had reached the young couple before their departure next morning) . . .

These thoughts eddied and dissolved in the Doctor's mind. He was breathless and hot as he arrived at the block of flats. Entering the gloom, he wearily ran a hand over the brass plate stating his name and profession. The surface was scorching; it seemed to sear the words onto his vision. He could still read:

GENERAL PRACTITIONER

halfway up the stairs.

An instant later the nameplate dissolved into patches of lucent darkness. He seemed to see the Turk's brilliant eyes, then the fee of two new coins. Now not even Benchimol's failings could overlay the memory of how cursorily LeGrand had examined the body. He no longer told himself that the man was suffering from acute food poisoning; he forgot Daniel's alleged reluctance to forsake his hotel for the Arab quarter.

At what point he had admitted to himself the true diagnosis, the Doctor could no longer remember. But finding himself incapable of rallying Benchimol's shortcomings, he observed himself, as if from a distance, trying to maintain that one case of cholera would not lead to an epidemic, and that he need not alert the hospital or police.

Chapter 9

The organ continued playing though the service had ended. Its festive peals filled the basilica like bells. The saints and martyrs, all severe in the brilliant blues, greens, and golds of their victory, stared down from the candle-lit dome. Below them the convent procession filed into the nearby refectory. It stopped at regular intervals as each nun knelt before the altar, and walked on, returning her eyes to the ground.

Only the silver haired man, one of whose hands fitted loosely into the front of his white waistcoat, did not genuflect as he moved into the aisle. He followed two priests and a fat gentleman who had also occupied the visitors' stalls at the back. The gentleman turned to offer the support of his arm; but the old man continued to stand apart, possibly through uncertainty. He was gazing at the great crucifix: it was suspended from the darkness. Looking down to the flower-decked altar he noticed a picture of someone serenely exposing his heart.

As M. Grimaud walked on, he recalled that when he had received a letter with the words *Convent of the Sacred Heart* punched onto the back of the envelope, he had not opened it until he finished his morning coffee. He knew that all the sanatorium bills were paid; he doubted whether he, or his offspring, was being claimed for the

Order. The old man turned instead to a letter from Benchimol.

Setting aside the new clause of their contract, enclosed for his signature, he read Giselle's neatly-penned pages. (It was she who had been writing for some weeks now.) Daniel and she wanted to call M. Grimaud's godson 'Solomon', but the adoption rules were strict: the child must retain his own name. Yet they were certain that he would find young Gilles adorable. Giselle was even sure that she had been called 'Mamma'.

Grimaud imagined her carrying the baby in her arms. Doubtless she would be as nervous that Gilles would hurt himself as Ivette had been with Albert. They would have to move all porcelain and crystal well out of his reach. The Benchimols surely had a beautiful home.

'Come and stay for as long as you like.' She wrote it for the second time. The rooms which M. Grimaud would use had been decorated with floral wallpapers specially ordered from England. In the afternoons, Giselle went on, she would read to him among the orchids in the solarium.

'Yes,' the old man thought to himself, folding the letter. He and Daniel's wife (like his own) had taken a strong liking to each other on first meeting. He had never been to Lyons. They might take carriage rides in the surrounding country. After all, what was there to stop him? . . .

Grimaud's fragile early-morning calm was shattered by Albert leaning over the upstairs banister, one cheek still covered in shaving soap. He wanted to know the time. The boy disturbed his father again, a few minutes later. For on inquiring, and being told, why there was a letter from the Convent, he said:

'You're not going, I hope. A Jew like you can't start celebrating Christian festivals!'

'Why "like me"? Besides, they're only nuns. D'you suppose they intend to eat me?' . . .

By now Grimaud had followed the procession into the refectory. The sisters were standing silently by the long candle-lit tables. A heavy scent of datura wafted through the open windows from the cloister garden. Grimaud was placed next to the Mother Superior, back from the sanatorium for All Souls' Day, at a table horizontal to and slightly higher than the rest. She smiled at him reassuringly before ringing a small bell. Her quiet, audible voice chanted the Latin grace. Outside in the kitchen Arabic was being spoken.

Grimaud found the rituals somewhat disconcerting. Perhaps the strange language and gestures used by everyone except him—even LeGrand was now crossing himself at the opposite side of the table—left him feeling conspicuous. (He tried, though with what success he could not tell, to preserve the detached dignity of an observer.) Or was it the suspicion of hectic piety which had somehow alarmed him? The crucifixes and pietas surely rendered the suffering too brazen.

Having sat down, the Mother Superior asked Grimaud:

'How is Albert?' She spoke as if she had always known his son. Most people of his acquaintance would have made the question sound trivial or falsely confidential; either would have simply been a use of the boy as a means of inaugurating an inevitable social conversation. But the Mother Superior—her tone even and low, her features clean-cut yet smooth as ivory—had always seemed to apprehend the complexities summoned forth by her remarks. And waiting for the answers, she had appeared unperturbed by the passage of time.

'He's very well.' She continued looking at Grimaud, expecting his defensive statement to give way to a fuller reply.

Her eyes really *were* extraordinary. He felt them penetrate without prying; anticipate without badgering; understand without judging. Above all, he imagined that she saw the things about which inarticulateness or inhibition prevented him from speaking. Some power dissolved the flesh and blood which normally concealed his heart.

'I don't seem to see much of him these days. He

spends a great deal of time with a young lady.' Noticing her ring, he wondered if she had ever contemplated marriage. In her white habit she seemed less old than was usual for one in her position. Grimaud found youthfulness intimidating when combined with such authority.

'That's natural at his age. What is he? About twenty?'

Remembering the girl in her long, light dresses, Grimaud regretted that she was such an infrequent guest in his home. He understood all too well that Albert had no wish for him to meet Catherine; the boy positively scowled when his father grew expansive in his conversation on the day that she met the Benchimols at lunch. Even so, surely Grimaud still retained the right to entertain whom he pleased in his own house.

He knew that the villa lacked the feminine charm with which Ivette had once filled it. There were only flowers when he remembered to ask the gardener to cut them; he forgot to supervise the polishing of the furniture, and in consequence the marquetry surfaces of some fine pieces had buckled and cracked. However there was a superb view: you could see the greater part of Stanley Bay.

Grimaud would have enjoyed female company. He missed the soft voices, the smooth hair, the cool skin. Only occasionally, smoking in the study or suffering from insomnia, would he hear light footsteps.

'Is that you, son?'

'Yes . . . Goodnight.' Was there also the movement of silk?

Grimaud would picture Catherine's eyes: they were doe-like and dark. Beneath an apparent composure he sensed a fretful tension which (like Ivette) she would try to undo by interlacing and unlocking her fingers.

On the moonlit lawn, visible from an upstairs lavatory window, Grimaud sometimes saw two figures ambling and talking. They would stand apart, holding hands. But then the sea, which had sparkled between them, appeared to lessen and shrink. It was displaced by a single form: it might quiver for minutes at a time . . .

'And who is your son's young lady-friend, if I may

ask?' Grimaud was stirred from his thoughtfulness by a Spanish sister, the novice mistress, sitting at his other side. As she spoke the more luxuriant hairs of her incipient moustache vibrated on a ball of fat.

'I believe her name is Catherine.'

'Ah! One of our saint's names.' Grimaud almost countered by saying that far from being a Papist, or indeed a Christian at all, the girl was partially Arab. But on reflecting that the Sister would derive hardly less satisfaction from learning that his Jewish son acted as consort to a Muslim than she had from thinking Catherine a Catholic, he looked down, chewed and pretended, an index-finger raised, that no matter how the nun wished to behave, no gentleman would talk with his mouth full.

In the strained silence that followed—both the Sister and he felt pangs of remorse at robbing the other of victory—Grimaud's mind started wandering again. He rubbed his eyes; they were tired. He remembered lying in bed, hearing the conversation floating up from the lawn. By now the two figures were so far away, perhaps by the low terracotta wall overlooking the Bay at the perimeter of the garden, that their words were quite indistinct. Grimaud only made out the tones of the voices: they were soft, urgent, and spasmodic. He tried to listen more carefully, as he used to as a small boy, overhearing sounds from the impenetrable world of his parents.

But would that racket never end? (He must have dozed off.) Although the two of them were speaking so loudly, he did not know what they were saying. Surely they realized that an invalid needed his rest. The least they could do was to sit with him. On and on the conversation continued.

Eventually, not knowing how often he had been woken, Grimaud told himself that he should never tolerate such behaviour. His son on the lawn with a young lady, unescorted, in the small hours of the morning: it was a situation which no father should countenance!

Standing at his window, Grimaud knocked on the glass,

but without eliciting a response from the garden. He rapped until he could no longer bear the pain in his knuckles. Peering at the eucalyptus and mulberry trees, he heard the wind displacing their foliage: his son was coughing next door in his sleep.

Had he merely imagined the noises? Perhaps he had hallucinated them; LeGrand was prescribing him laudanum recently. Besides, what was wrong with showing concern for one's son? Nobody but another parent could understand a father's interest in his only child.

Unable to sleep at all now, he lay thinking. He recalled times when Albert had eaten, his brow wrinkled, not wishing to talk. Grimaud wanted to stroke the tension away from the boy's forehead. He would gladly have suffered this upheaval for him, shown him that no matter how overwhelming his problems appeared at the moment they would seem less pressing in time. Yet the old man knew that his son would push his fingers away. For Albert, feeling that his father minimized his emotions, also resented all interference with his life by someone who had made such a conspicuous failure of his own. So Grimaud sighed, scarcely looking up from the newspaper. There he read of Arabi's latest demands. (How he had disliked his own father's indifference: the old man read all his correspondence at meals.)

It was sad, Grimaud thought, still tossing and turning, that Albert was so brusque and self-absorbed. If only he was more open to other people's advice and experience he might take measures to avert an emotional catastrophe. Certainly Grimaud felt no wish to stamp out his son's tender emotions for Catherine; he knew the strength of such early loves. Nor did he harbour ill-feelings against the young lady. She was no more nervous or anaemic than many of her contemporaries. It was just that their friendship, rather over two years old, showed every sign of continuing, even growing. And with his absence of objectivity and perspective (natural in youth), Albert could not anticipate the disastrous consequences of marrying an Arab.

Eventually the objects in Grimaud's bedroom clarified out of amorphous, dark masses. The stays in a pair of shoes, the wood carving on a wardrobe, and the flower pattern around a china water pitcher: they were defined by a grey light. While outside, like a mocking reminder of the noise which had inspired his discomfort, there were the grating sounds of birds on the lawn.

Drifting, dazed, through the morning, and feeling robbed of his night's sleep, Grimaud often rested after lunch. Waking refreshed a few hours later, he watched the sea breezes rocking the palms in the garden. He sat beneath them in a silk dressing-gown, sipping iced tea.

Now it would be possible to think about Albert more coolly. He might even find the detachment to consider his son's unuttered recriminations. Surely the boy secretly suspected him of weakness and jealousy; Grimaud had noticed the reproach in his eyes. But with his worthless arm and fading eyesight, his lack of ambition and in-difference to the future, the old man hardly rebuked him-self for his occasional envy of the young. For their physical prowess and thirst for experience, their excite-ment at the variousness of life and belief in its benignity, had inspired wonder no less than other more negative reactions . . .

Grimaud was roused by the silver bell. As he stood listening to grace, surprised at the dispatch with which they had eaten dinner, the events which he had been remembering seemed curiously distant. He had forgotten them altogether by the time they had moved to a long room for coffee. Light flickered over the marble floor; it settled in patches on the Mother Superior's forehead and cheeks.

'D'you think your son intends to marry Catherine?' Grimaud and the Mother Superior were standing apart from the others. Her question startled him. He realized that she was continuing the same conversation as before, unruffled by his curt replies and lengthy silence.

'I'm not certain what his plans are.' He ran his fingers through the tip of his straggling beard. Then, as if he had not already answered: 'I don't see how he could. She's an Arab.' For a moment he was aware of the remoteness of the other sisters and guests.

'It could have been worse. She might have been born a Catholic.' Surely she was teasing him about his quarrel with the Spanish Sister. 'But wouldn't one of us have made an acceptable daughter-in-law?' Turning away, almost shocked by her playfulness, Grimaud heard her go on: 'Of course, I know it must be very complicated.' He was glad of the reprieve.

Later they strolled after the other nuns, towards the cloister. Grimaud was talking about his affection for Paris. (The Mother Superior, seeking to further relieve the tension caused by her bantering remarks, had been asking when Albert hoped to leave for his studies at the Sorbonne.) Grimaud tried to explain his love for the city with references to buildings, art galleries, restaurants, and past events. He was almost conscious of excising any reminiscence which could not have been printed in a guide-book; his nervousness made the description stilted, he knew.

As they drew towards the end of the room the Mother Superior paused at the door opening onto the garden. Grimaud, having preceded her, turned back: he sensed that she wished to speak to him.

Before them the cloister, its stones still warm from the day, seemed to confine a square of stars. While rising up from the dusty earth, as if deprived of the space in which to grow, an olive tree writhed in the dark.

'I wonder, M. Grimaud, whether you know why most people join our Convent,' the Mother Superior began inconsequentially. 'You may find it difficult to believe, but they choose to. I expect you've heard tales of the queens and princesses who were forced to enter closed Orders because their brothers or cousins thought it would be politically convenient. Perhaps you think we're all here for our looks.' He glanced away from her even features. 'Yet on the whole we aren't sent here by our families or relatives. We've usually looked forward to entering the Convent, for whatever reasons, and are pleased to leave the world behind. I remember when I joined I thought nothing of sacrificing the excitement of living in a big city such as Paris. The food, the society, the culture which you were describing, seemed no loss when set against the quiet and dedication of the Order. But I was young in those days.' She paused. 'And in time, far from finding the quiet and dedication which I expected, I became unsettled and turbulent. In fact,' she was looking out at the gnarled olive stump, 'I felt so discontented that I began to think of the Convent as a form of confinement. It was a prison from which I longed to escape. Although I had come here of my own free will, I imagined that I was being detained, like the ugly daughters and princesses of history. Some wicked relation seemed to have stolen the world from me, despite the fact that I no longer had any family. And so, outside our walls, I pictured nothing but dinner-parties from which the host was always excluding me, and marriages in which someone else was always being chosen as the bride.'

The Mother Superior fell silent for a moment, considering. 'I'm sure, M. Grimaud, that you must be wondering why I'm telling you all this. After all, you doubtless know that we rarely speak of ourselves.' Breaking in on his conventional remark about quite understanding, she continued: 'It's just that in time my bitterness and envy lessened. I can't say how or when it began to do so. Here,' she gazed around her, 'we should probably interpret it as the intervention of Divine grace. But you see, it was as if I began to realize that in reality I had no tormentor. No one was cheating me out of my life. And I grew to accept, equally slowly, that my daily existence had not been plundered of its promise or riches. It had only seemed sterile because I had been so busy inventing imaginary bandit-relations that I never had time to look for the treasures buried under the surface.'

They passed into the cloister. The Doctor, slightly tipsy, was surrounded by a group of young nuns. He was explaining—not for the first time that evening—that a cholera epidemic, once confined, must grow worse before improving. Several sisters were practising a part-song beneath the datura. Outside there was the drone of Arabs celebrating a Ramadan night. The Mother Superior turned back for the last time.

'Our lives, M. Grimaud, cannot be stolen so easily; not by our mothers or fathers—still less by our sons.'

PART III
Weeks Later

Marriage and Other Contracts

Chapter 10

The guests were leaving. They called back up the steps to the lighted porch where Catherine and her family were standing.

'Goodnight, and thank you again for a wonderful evening. You must be terribly excited. If I were in your place I wouldn't be able to sleep a wink tonight!'

Girls in long dresses, slim fans dangling from their gloved wrists, were helped into coaches. The servants, who patiently held lamps during the lengthy departure, watched the agitated flight of moths, attracted from the garden, with remote but unflinching eyes.

'Don't go yet. Stay a few minutes longer,' Catherine whispered to Albert as the maid approached with his hat and cane.

'I'll wait until most of the others have left.'

They stood, only the backs of their hands touching. The movement of carriages and friends never disrupted the calm rise and fall of their identical breathing; and the sounds of their own voices, returning greetings through the darkness, seemed emptied of substance to them.

Sometimes in the past when they had looked at the sea, not speaking for minutes at a time, Albert seemed to lose all sense of being separate from Catherine. He would stare at the black water, gradually feeling the usual limits of his personality eroded by the constant ebbing and flowing. His heart, forsaking its normal rhythm, beat as if every vein and artery were emptying into the fingers extended beside him. Turning to press against her soft mass, Albert's shaking body no longer preserved its definite contours. It merged into Catherine's —until she stiffened and holding him back said:

'I love you.'

They began to talk, walking the whole length of M. Grimaud's garden. Albert pulled blossoms from trees and gave them to Catherine with the seriousness of symbolic gestures. She spoke of their future together, of the unbearable emptiness she would feel if he ever left her. And changing the subject after a moment of tension in their tightly clasped hands, she discussed the forthcoming party at which they hoped to announce their engagement.

'We'll invite everyone. It'll be the grandest party Alexandria has ever seen. My mother's already been giving me ideas for my dress.'

Catherine continued, saying that they should ask few people older than themselves; but Albert did not reply. He simply seemed to be listening. (He would often grow unaccountably strange and fall into a lengthy silence.) But, as it happened, he heard barely a word, despite his occasional monotone signs of interest. His attention was arrested by something Catherine had said earlier.

'If you ever left me I wouldn't want to go on living.'

He felt the same. He could not conceive of a life that was not spent together. Every parting, no matter how trivial, filled him with crippling anxiety. Even at the start of each meeting he already felt the cold shadow cast by the departure. Then, insecure about a future which he rationally knew was unlikely to falter, Albert found himself speaking harshly to Catherine:

'Don't keep chattering all the time. Go home! You're giving me a headache.' He wrinkled his brow and put a tired hand to his eyes.

Now, why had he said that? There was no reason for such brutality. She was staring at him with a mixture

171

of incomprehension and tenderness turning to pain. The last thing Albert wanted was to hurt her; for her to go; for her to leave him. He did not know how he would survive the hour after if she took him at his word and went away.

Catherine put out her hand. It was usually she who first tried to end their quarrels. He could smell her perfume, the musky scent of her hair. And as she stroked his wrist, he sensed the presence of a smooth body beyond her cuffs and below her neckline. Naturally, he had never seen it. But he knew it well from his fantasies, and by innumerable silk folds.

How he wished they could be together without her eventually whispering:

'No, Albert, don't,' as his hand travelled to the forbidden places. She always stiffened and grew sensible just when he wanted her most. If only Catherine could know that she was indispensable to his very existence. His life before their encounter now seemed an uninhabitable waste.

Yet lowering his head as he witnessed her smoothing his palm, and unable to see where, or how, to start representing feelings whose relief demanded description, Albert suddenly pulled away his hand. He stood apart, watching the water. He despaired of ever behaving in a way consistent with what he spontaneously felt.

After a while they walked again. Nothing was said for some time. The waves, and the leaves, and the rattling of an upstairs window were the only disturbances or sounds. Then, when Albert's breathing had steadied, he tried to explain what he could scarcely describe. He alluded to uncontrollable feelings which choked his true impulses to love.

So often he wanted to be tender; he needed to show affection and warmth. But the security he felt in her presence was undermined by dark fears, and black moods. He was afraid he would lose her; that she would leave him; that his personality was insipid and morose. He would never marry; he was unattractive; women surely found him implausible and immature. And then, he explained, his whitened knuckles digging into the palm of a hand, all this rising self-hatred would collect about one of Catherine's chance remarks. Her very patience and vulnerability attracted an irresistible pang of cruelty. There were wells of pure weakness in her large and beautiful eyes.

Afterwards, Albert's remorse excited even greater self-disgust. He was shocked by his own harshness and the arbitrary targets it chose. Of course Catherine would forgive him. She had always done so. But he noticed her observing his creeping self-pity with a detachment, polite but appalled.

As he continued talking a sentimental tone overtook his remarks. He was sure that it deprived his ostensible sufferings of their savage immediacy and pain. He could tell from the way Catherine was still looking, that they seemed melodramatic and unreal. Lamenting the difficulty of portraying one's feelings to others they even dissolved at her touch.

Now there was no further reason to speak of emotions with which he hardly credited himself. Like the clouds that crossed the moon's surface, they were evanescent and quite without form.

A warm wind was rising. Stray fragrances rode in the air. Leaves trembled from branches and landed on the flower beds and grass. For some reason Albert's breathing had quickened; his face was flushed; he could not stand still. It all happened in an instant. He embraced and hugged Catherine, kissing her on the backs of her hands and neck.

It was absurd that he should choose to argue when he could find fulfilment with such ease. Outside her arms nothing existed. Together everything was complete. It seemed that all the restless frustration which had characterized a commonplace world was over-ridden by a feeling of wholeness: it rendered life vivid and real. This was what things were really like: brilliant and vibrant and glad. Why dwell on the grey light over one's shoulder, or the beggar picking his fleas at one's door?

'The time will come,' he remembered Aunt Stella saying in the days when they lived together—he pictured her nodding in the darkness, stirring an empty coffee cup—'when you will meet a young lady, and your heart will go poum-poum-poum.' She knocked on her breast and added, smiling: 'Then you'll know that it's love. You will only have eyes for each other. There'll be no one in the world except you two.' She leant back in her chair, quivering. 'I know. I speak from experience . . . Now where did I put my glasses? Ah! Thank you. I don't know what I'd do without you.' And after a pause, during which she fingered her wedding ring abstractedly, she had added: 'But then that's young love . . .'

Albert was roused from these thoughts by his fiancée drawing her fingers away from his hand. As she waved to the last vehicle, halting at the foot of the steps, he reflected that his moods and anxieties had seemed quite remote at this evening's engagement party. The two ladies in the carriage were waiting for an old gentleman, one of Catherine's innumerable uncles, to be carried down in his wheel-chair. The butler snapped his fingers at two serving-boys playing hide-and-seek in the hall. Then scolding them for inattention, he directed the precarious descent.

The old man peered down at the moving stairway, hiccuping with the effects of champagne. He tried to call out to the happy couple, but his greetings were dyspeptic and unheard.

Catherine had turned from the marble portico and, rubbing her arms, sent the maid in for her shawl. She paused in the hallway until the servant returned, watching Albert staring across the wide lawn. Even in her wrap she did not move inward, but observed him for a moment or so more. He continued gazing into the darkness, past the gas lamps fixed to the wall.

Through the trees he could see, broken up into small pieces, the Ras-el-Tin Palace massed on a rise. Its great walls appeared like diamonds and spangles. In a central colonnade there were lights. A sentry caught the moon on his bayonet. Seconds later he recaptured it—or it could have been someone else. And a crescent fluttered over the garden from a flagpole. Peacock fans swept from branches away into the dark.

There was nothing which could detract from such splendour. Albert had often seen it displayed. He knew the feeling of richness: it was life's true element and form. No one could restrain the swelling grandeur which inspired with the solemnity of prayer. Outside it, all was ignoble. Its dimension alone promised hope.

Albert often thought he possessed the access, as vague energies rose within him and soared, to a strange sanctuary of life-force. It connected him with limitless power. He dared imagine great achievements; great enterprises might grow from his will. He knew heroes' immortal longings. There was no action which he might not perform.

He was immune to the weakness of others. Their fears made them petty and frail. He had seen mature men like Benchimol fret with worry. Would his business be disrupted by the renewed rioting? Would his offices be broken into? After all, were the Arabs not reacting violently against the quarantine imposed on them during the cholera epidemic?

And below the mound, which underlay the Palace, Albert noticed harbour lights shining through the trees. Large wooden crates, containing horses, double-beds and grand pianos, were hoisted onto ships which set sail even at night.

For weeks now Albert had seen Europeans afraid to go out without a military escort. They booked the first passage possible at shipping agencies on the Rue Rosette. Nervous men would wipe perspiration from their necks as the clerk announced that all places were taken for the immediate future. They might try to loosen a collar stud when frustrated in making arrangements for their furniture to be sent on in advance.

A friend had recently asked Albert to lunch. The invitation came as a surprise. For although the troubles had made European—and especially Jewish—families more intimate with each other, Albert had never received an invitation to the young man's house in Ramleh before.

The father, his eyes inflamed with dark pouches beneath them, indicated cushions, arranged around plates on the floor. The mother, helped by her twelve-year-old daughter, carried boiled eggs from the kitchen through the bare rooms. She did not arrange her skirts when she squatted, or tell her husband that yoke was dripping from his spoon onto his frock-coat.

Afterwards they looked through the French windows at the harbour. Despite the steamy panes the glass doors were kept closed. They discussed their place on the shipping company's waiting list. The sun's outline was entirely lost in the heat. But even so, the white haze over the water did not obscure the continual activity down by the port.

'Your father has a few boats, doesn't he, Albert?' M. Gabai asked the question adjusting his crackling money-belt, staring down at the cargo and cranes. Doubtless he intended to sound nonchalant, speaking lightly of the central point of their meeting, as Albert knew any experienced businessman would. But his hands were clenched, and his face, forming the focus for all his family's attention, grew suddenly rigid and intense. Incapable of affecting unconcern any longer, he turned to Albert with a twitching right eye and cheek.

'Not now. I think he sold them all to a businessman from Lyons called . . .'

'Not all,' M. Gabai interrupted, pacing around the debris of cushions and egg shells. 'We've discovered that two were never sold.' As his wife stood in the hallway gesturing to the children to follow her into another room, Albert noticed a small wooden cylinder, containing a scroll inscribed with part of the Talmud, pinned to the door-post.

'A number of us,' Gabai continued, walking, 'have

been able to read the signs of the times. Plague, riots, fighting—these things aren't simply accidents you know. They're all part of a plan. Our life here is finished. It's clear.' He waved back the air. 'We must move on, begin again, leave Egypt. After all there are good precedents.' He gave a grim smile.

'Now I know that your father hasn't been very well lately.' He put an arm on Albert's shoulder. 'That's why I invited you here today to lunch.' Looking sternly at the young man, he added confidentially: 'We need those ships—both of them. Do you think you could persuade him to sell?'

The interview only lasted a few minutes longer. Gabai regretted that the price they could offer was not high. But he felt sure that M. Grimaud would be sympathetic to any project which would help advance Zionism. He could scarcely imagine that with Albert's influence he would refuse.

Mme Gabai took Albert's hand as he was leaving.

'God will repay you,' she said. 'And take care.'

'Don't forget,' a voice called when he was already in the garden, 'stress the historic role.'

Albert turned and saw Mme Gabai standing by the window. She was watching him walk down the drive while a figure, gesticulating with no visible interlocuter, was still pacing in the half-light inside.

Away across the city Albert was able to see the Arab quarter as he made his way home from the Gabais' house. A shelf of low cloud reddened by the sunset hovered over the dense mass of streets. On the side near the harbour, where cordons had been set up by the police, torn sheets, yellowed and sagging with the humidity, signalled quarantine from the windows of huts.

Egyptians broke out of their confinement at all times of the day. There were many points at which they could climb onto a low roof and drop down into quiet European streets. Only a few days before, Albert had heard Benchimol telling his father, a celebrated French contralto, dressing for a recital, had unexpectedly confirmed her professional reputation by reaching second C as she noticed a young man stealing across her hotel veranda. Arabs might bribe the guards, often cousins, or claim to be carrying goods for merchants going into the city daily with legitimate passes. It seemed improbable that even Alexandria contained sufficient cafés and restaurants to employ the endless lines of waiters who presented themselves, morning and evening, all dressed in fezs, wing collars, and black ties.

Albert, like most Europeans, soon recognized that the measures taken to combat cholera were proving ineffective. The doctors' insistence on confining the epidemic was no more than a counsel of perfection. Anyone who had been unfortunate enough to cross the Arab quarter, before or during the crisis, had seen naked girls, their hair clotted with reddish mud, excreting in the streets; or beggars picking rotten fruit from drains through which brown rats had dragged their enormous pelts. They might well be sceptical of attempts to purify the Egyptian water supply and control its sewerage system.

Besides, the Arabs had little desire to help themselves. They seemed temperamentally incapable of facing the facts of the situation. In the *pâtisserie* which Albert sometimes visited, the sons of prosperous Egyptian businessmen, living in big houses remote from the quarantined parts of the city, claimed that there was no sickness or epidemic. They talked wildly, almost shouting, when Albert insisted on mentioning the cart-loads of wasted bodies buried each evening at Chatby. They claimed his attention by squeezing his forearm so tightly that he was only just able to raise his chocolate cup without wincing. Did he not know that cholera was merely a convenient Imperialist excuse for isolating the Arab community? It was a means of cutting Arabi off from his Nationalist supporters, of depriving his party of its legitimate political power.

When Arabs did admit that there were perhaps cases of illness, they said that they were only to be found among the European population. After all, it was well known that the first outbreaks had occurred in Camp Caesar and Ramleh. Why then should Egyptians be discriminated against when the French and English had been responsible for spreading disease?

Albert could barely imagine that Arabs believed their own arguments. Surely they were sceptical of the rabble-rousers' opinions which they were constantly repeating. For cynical politicians were prepared to seize any opportunity, no matter how far fetched, to incense an ignorant people against the Jewish community.

In effect, Arabi and his so-called 'Nationalist' party licensed terrorism with their rallies and speeches. Personal property was no longer held sacred; family life was continually disrupted; while one's bodily safety was endangered countless times every day.

Albert continued looking down at the mud huts and alleys as he walked home from M. Gabai's house. They merged into the surrounding dark. Even grey gulls, shrieking as they circled over the damp quarter and dockyard, were gathered up by a blackening sky.

Albert imagined a shadowy figure with glistening eyes jumping from a narrow window. Landing in a private road, where night robbed the clumps of carnations and pinks growing beside a villa of their ragged edges and colour, the youth entered a lighted room, carrying something of the darkness in with him.

Eerier images rose up in Albert's mind. Amorphous black shapes grew out of an obscure, shifting centre. They expanded and swelled, seeming to overwhelm the surrounding patches. Submerging nearby parts, previously grey and reminiscent of twilight, the malignant progress threatened to become so rapid and complete that Albert caught himself staring blankly around and gulping the air in large, confused mouthfuls.

No, they must be kept back at all costs! They must not be allowed to break loose and enter the restricted areas. Then slowly, in time, life would perhaps grow more normal. Sitting relaxed, one might forget the tension and strain; and eventually, with danger at bay, one could lose sight of the fear of the times altogether.

But to achieve that—Albert braced himself and walked smartly—to ensure that degree of tranquillity and composure one needed great strength. One required will-power to over-ride opposition. An unembarrassed force of personality was indispensable to success.

Moreover, one would have to isolate oneself from all insecurity. No leader could extend his dominion without becoming insensitive to doubt. Weakness too should be expected even from those closest to one. Albert saw the need to treat their timidity with imperious disdain.

It was, after all, not everyone who had the resources to make momentous decisions. Only some, like Gabai—and even he had scarcely concealed his agitation a few hours earlier—formulated the issues correctly. The majority were incapable of performing actions which would anticipate the inevitable processes of history.

What was needed now was not timidity acquiescing in the face of growing danger. To stay at home, afraid of visiting friends or even riding through the city in the evening, was not a regime to which Albert, who was neither an invalid nor ancient, would ever submit.

The moon was hidden by trees, when Albert paused to open the gates to their villa. Foliage, limp with moisture, rustled for the first time for days. And beyond the six columns a single light glowed from an upstairs room. For a moment Albert thought he caught sight of an Imperial pavilion. As he entered, the yellowish glow elevated a sphynx and marble cheek to his notice.

Surely there was here the cool atmosphere of sacro-sanctity. Silence dispersed all associations which might have made the walled space familiar. And even the remaining image—of Gabai's house, hot and emptied of furniture—contrived to heighten the awful impression, by contrast, in Albert's mind.

'Is that you, son?'

Albert paused in the hall, unable, and unwilling, to

lose touch with such sacred sensations. His fingers clasped the powerful form of a lion's gold paws. Gazing into the penumbra, his eyes seemed to make contact with the stern expression of M. Grimaud's father. It stared from the canvas, out through the open study.

'Who's there? Is that you, Albert?'

He sighed and turned to the staircase.

'Yes, it's me.' Between the metal rungs he was able to see the ends of a beard, framed by part of a bedroom door. Its white whisps, glittering with sweat, were jaundiced by the lamp light. Then the strands attached to a chin; a lean jaw; there were colourless lips. They appeared to mouth words. Albert observed the peering eyes as his footsteps carried him above the level of the banister.

The face continued to scrutinize as he emerged from the dark. A wave of tired air, of surgical spirit and laundry, wafted away from the bedroom.

'Albert?' The old man suspiciously repeated the question.

Albert lingered by the door. He would probably have to stay for no more than the few minutes he spent several times weekly. Yet his father, whom he had simply not seen for nearly two days, seemed less resigned and withdrawn than usual. With a tray of biscottes and thick soup, largely untouched, set apart on the nearby rumpled bedclothes, and magazines and books heaped in disorder by his chair, Grimaud abruptly pulled a stifling travelling rug away from his legs. And then, sitting in his damp pyjamas, he continued the fidgeting which had grown compulsive with the unrelieved humidity of the day.

Outside the wind was now rising. It entered beneath doors and through windows, filling the hallway and stairs. Carrying the hems of silk curtains before it, it scattered newspapers into sheets.

'I was wondering who it was,' Grimaud said once again, straining to see into the agitated darkness. Even the hairs on his beard were disturbed.

He suddenly shot back in his chair and sat upright. Trembling, his head did not turn as both eyes searched the air. A shutter had sprung loose from its catch somewhere below them. It battered against the wall.

'You shouldn't be out at this time of night. They say there's been a lot of violence lately.'

'I can take care of myself,' Albert answered, beginning to slouch off. A step or so further up the corridor he continued: 'Anyhow, it's not really so late.' He immediately regretted having said so.

'Isn't it?' His father's answer was instant. Pulling a watch from his pyjamas top pocket, Grimaud fixed Albert with a prolonged side-long glance. He only interrupted his stare for a token look at the time piece. And replacing the watch, with a practised, though somewhat trembling, wrist action, he had also returned the glance. Indeed Albert, who had succeeded in walking no further, felt that the eyes never left him—not even when his father, yawning, passed a hand over his face. 'I'm exhausted. I feel as though I'd been waiting up half the night.'

'But that's the whole point, Papa. I don't want you to wait up for me. You should have been in bed hours ago. Remember what the Doctor said about building up your reserves of energy.'

'You don't understand. I can't sleep without knowing whether you're safe or . . .' Grimaud's body tautened, stopping the words in his mouth with a gasp. The wind had again dashed the shutter against the outside of the house. It banged several times more, and a further shutter joined the unpredictable battering. 'These days anything could happen and it might be hours before I was notified.'

'You worry too much. You always imagine the worst. Life can't just stop because of the troubles. Can't you see, it simply does no good to give in to these people? We must all try to go on living just the same.'

'Ha!' Grimaud gave a bitter, mock laugh. With his writhing fingers and fretful expression, it seemed to release a fraction of his long-constricted emotions. 'As if it were possible not to be anxious when you never tell me where you're going or how long you'll be.'

'Well it's my life. I'm entitled to do what I want with it.'

Albert distanced himself from his father. He took a further few steps into the corridor. Yet feeling vulnerable at his back to the old man's reproachful stare, he turned and noticed Grimaud's giant shadow, cast on the bedroom wall. Looking at the head with its exaggerated eye sockets and cheek cavities, at the enlarged knuckles terminating the chair arms like a pair of great claws, he went on:

'I refuse to be judged by you! I don't have to render account!' He found that he was shouting at the looming shape which presided over the echoes and darkness.

'Naturally not. I'm merely your father. I must keep quiet when I see you ruining your own future.'

'Really! You're becoming rather melodramatic, aren't you? You know very well that I'm not ruining anything at all.'

'Do I?' Grimaud's voice was rising. He moved forward. Albert could no longer see the shadow. There was only his father's gaunt head. 'I know more of what's going on than you think. As far as you're concerned I'm just an old invalid. But I have eyes. I can see everything that's happening.'

'Such as what?' Albert demanded. He strode back into the bedroom.

'I think you know. Your friends.' Grimaud paused, his lips hinting at the remarks which he did not choose to make. 'Arabs.' He allowed himself the word with distaste.

'Arabs? What Arabs?'

'You're blinded to it now,' his father began, his voice a little more blank, 'but I assure you that you'll never be happy with her.' His dull tone was the price he paid for emptying his speech of the emotions which might have made him seem less infallible.

'Who, Catherine? But she's not an Arab.'

'You see! You think I'm ignorant and stupid.' Grimaud's face beamed, sarcastic with triumph. 'But there are some things which even a living corpse like your old father knows better than you. Despite your *immense* maturity and experience, you never bothered to find out that she's practically an Arab.'

'Her name isn't "she",' Albert snapped. 'It's "Catherine". And in any case she isn't an Arab.'

'But her grandmother was.' Grimaud affected an air of tired patience. 'I knew her myself. I'm afraid, son, that you're sadly ignorant of the basic facts of the case.'

'Since when was one's grandmother half of the family? Besides, I'm not the one who's ignorant. Catherine's grandmother, as you should have remembered if you knew her'—Albert inclined his head, as though to a troublesome child—'was a Jewess from Upper Egypt . . .'

'An Arab . . .' Grimaud shouted over the crash of the shutters.

'An Arab-Jewess!' They continued their banging. 'And please don't interrupt me when I'm talking.'

'Really!' Grimaud turned and, with a mixture of self-pity and anger, gazed at the family photographs standing on the bedside table. 'If your grandfather or mother could hear you speaking to your own father like this.'

'She was an Arab-Jewess, as I was saying. Doubtless you've heard that the Jews living in Nubia and Luxor . . .'

'. . . are strictly Arabs . . .' As he called out above the continual battering, Grimaud noticed his wife and himself, faded and framed, on honeymoon by the Bosphorus. He was wearing the fez which they all wore.

'. . . are strictly Jews! They're descendants of the original, pre-Turkish, inhabitants of Egypt, who were never converted to Islam. They practised a primitive form of Judaism . . .'

'. . . which makes her an Arab.' Grimaud traced a quivering arc with his hand, emphasizing, with its supposed elegance, the inevitable logic of his oft-repeated conclusion.

'If anything, it makes her an Egyptian-Jewess. But you know very well that you're only trying to distort the facts!'

'Listen, Albert.' His son opened his mouth to interject. 'Now listen to me for a moment! I've lived longer than you; I've seen more of life.' His son was audibly sighing. 'And you may not choose to believe me, but it's nonetheless true that people such as these are simply not like us.' He raised an index finger, clearing the way for the rest of his laboured reasoning. 'I can see what this girl's like. She's dull—dead and dull. Of course, I know you're infatuated with her. I daresay, you even think you love her. But don't you see, that makes you the last person to understand what she's really like. I tell you,' and here the even tone strained, 'they have a closed view of the world. They're blinkered and narrow. They're inflexible, unwilling to change. She'll be a millstone—you mark my words. She'll drag you down with her dullness.'

Albert replied, brandishing a finger:

'I don't have to listen to your insults!' Then, taking a further step into the room, and holding his head high, he went on: 'Anyway, you've absolutely no basis for what you're saying. You've hardly ever even spoken to the lady.'

'I've hardly ever spoken to *the lady*.' Grimaud bowed his head with a sour, wrinkled smile, as he parodied his son. 'You really are quite the young gentleman! One might almost forget what goes on every evening by the trees. No wonder you want me to be in bed sleeping.'

'So you pry as well, do you, you vindictive old . . .' The shutters crashed again and again. Broken glass tinkled from one of the windows.

'Since matters have reached this point,' Albert said in a voice now so controlled that it had become almost formal, 'I think you might as well know that Catherine and I are going to get married—with, or without your permission. The wedding will be held before I leave for the Sorbonne. We intend to live in Paris.'

Grimaud did not seem to react. He simply sat looking

185

before him. Albert was not sure if his father had even heard the ultimatum. Only the wind, dispersing the fetid air and dampness, sounded above their irregular breathing.

After perhaps a minute and a half Albert found that he could endure his father's impassivity no longer: the old head appeared suddenly frail. Albert went on, in a voice which had grown almost kindly:

'Catherine's parents will be holding the engagement party in their house shortly. Do you think . . . I mean, do you think you will be free to attend?'

Albert's father was still bowing his head. It moved from side to side in his hands. It was impossible to tell whether he was answering the question, or responding to the demands of some inner voice. Suddenly, looking up with eyes that had grown hardened and flinty, he demanded:

'And how are you going to live? Where is your money going to come from?'

'We were hoping . . .' Albert's voice faltered, 'perhaps . . . that is, until I've graduated and begin my career, that we might be given—or at least borrow . . .'

'Don't tell me. I know the rest: "some money". And who do you expect the generous donor to be?'

'Well, Catherine's father has offered part, and we . . .'

'. . . want the rest from me, is that it?'

Albert did not reply. He stared at his father's eyes, hearing the jalousies beating the walls with a violence which seemed only to increase their fury.

'Even if I could give you the money I don't see why I should. As it is I've spent too much on you already. Your education alone has nearly broken me. Besides, I must consider my old age. I know very well that if you had your way you'd drain my last drop of blood and leave me to die in the gutter.'

'How can you say that? I've never asked you for money before. And what I've cost you in the past is what any father would spend . . .'

'But not on a son like you!' Grimaud pointed a bony finger and swallowed.

'But, Father, you're a rich man. You must have made a fortune out of selling the ships alone. You can well afford to be generous.'

'Generous!' Grimaud's fragile body shook. 'Since when have you been generous with me? You begrudge me every second of your time!'

'But you could sell the remaining ships,' Albert tried to go on reasoning, 'and help me without even touching your capital.'

'Who said anything about "remaining ships"?' Grimaud frowned.

'M. Gabai,' Albert answered nervously.

'I might have known it! You've been discussing my business with that vulgar little man. Well you and your friend might be interested to know that I've already promised the ships to Benchimol. Besides, if Gabai were the last Jew on earth . . .'

'You wouldn't just be helping M. Gabai though. If you were willing to sell,' Albert tentatively advanced, 'you'd be providing transport for the whole Jewish community.'

Grimaud looked at his son, amazed and perplexed.

'O-h!' He drew out the syllable in imitation of awe. 'I should be honoured to have a great man in my house! What a blessing that my offspring should be so visionary! What a curse'—his voice was now charged with anger and spite—'to have given birth to a person so low and so ruthless! Is nothing sacred to you? Not even your religion or people? You couldn't give a damn about the Jews or anyone else. You just want to use them to levy blood-money for your marriage.'

'That's unfair!' The rain was coming into the house. Large drops spattered the marble. 'You've always refused to believe in me for what I am.' Air, long confined, was agitated by new currents.

'What you are! I know what you are. You're hard— hard!' He banged the chair arm. 'If you really cared for your people you'd talk to me, sit with me sometimes.' He shouted above the noise of the thunder. 'I'm there to be made use of—to give. All you want is to exploit me. Can't you see? You're no better than these plundering savages. No wonder you're marrying into them.'

'But you've never given anything to me!' Their faces were made grotesque by the lightning. 'You've given everything you've got to Benchimol. It's a pity he isn't your son instead.'

'At least he wouldn't have been so ruthless and self-willed. Thank God that somebody still knows how to show affection.'

'He wouldn't have learnt it from you,' Albert shrieked. 'You killed my mother with your cruelty!'

Grimaud lurched forward. He struck Albert on the face. Even his right hand was clenched. He sank back in the chair. He was groaning.

It had gone on raining all night. The shutters banged; their hinges had continued their moaning . . .

Albert remembered, as he gazed at the harbour from Catherine's garden, how each thunderbolt had seemed to riddle his father's body with pain . . .

'Albert! Come in!' Catherine was calling. (The last guests had left.) British gunboats had opened fire. Their report could be heard throughout the dark city.

Chapter 11

There was less light than an hour ago. As he looked over her shoulder, protruding from the crude cover, Benchimol noticed that the window had grown as dark as the surrounding mud. Even his clothes, hurriedly hung over a nail on the back of the door, merged into the shadows. The stiff collar and crisp shirt front were indistinguishable from the sombre trousers and jacket.

She had simply thrown her dress onto the bed. It still lay there. He had watched her waiting as he removed his cuff links and undid the studs. Her breasts drooped.

He observed them without speaking. Then, despite all their previous meetings, the Arab girl gathered the silk to her bosom, like a forlorn baby. And with eyes that flinched before his continual attention, she had whispered, her head lowered:

'Shame.'

She always wore the same dress. (He withdrew his hand as the fingers touched it.) Originally it had belonged to Giselle. Daniel had rescued it from the parlourmaid's cupboard where it had awaited conversion into cleaning cloths and floor rags. Putting it into the concealed pouch of a valise which he took with him on his business trips to Egypt, once his wife had finished supervising the servant who was packing his case, he remembered Giselle wearing it as the hostess of their first ball in Lyons. Now he recalled the garden, fragrant with pine trees and roses . . . The frock bore the strong, unwashed odour of the girl's body. Its smell was scarcely obliterated by the heavy scent of sandalwood.

At first Daniel had been amused by the punctiliousness with which the girl would display his gifts whenever he visited her. She would no more have thought of receiving him in the tattered Muslim clothes worn by the older women lounging in the alleyway than of walking without the high-heeled pink slippers which were almost two sizes too big. Besides, he derived an odd sort of pleasure from diverting presents, which ingratiating clients requested him to convey to Mme Benchimol with their compliments, to the hands of an Egyptian whore of seventeen.

Giselle would have taken such good care of the embroidered handkerchiefs. They would have been put into drawers with *Roger et Gallet* soaps and sachets of lavender, never to be revealed unless other ladies, at coffee or in the next seat at the Opera, were there to admire them; while the folds of a Sevillian fan, hand painted with details from Goya's earlier work, might have been interleaved with tissue papers which would only have fluttered away when their adopted son Gilles married, or eventually came into his inheritance. As it was, the dark figure cast up in a blanket was disfigured by a tear which ran down most of his spine. The wooden ends, sticking through their silk coverings like ribs, had splintered and grown discoloured.

If Giselle could have seen the sorry thing now what would she have said? She was so neat; her home was in impeccable taste; she was such a good mother. Doubtless she would have considered it a form of sacrilege to abandon the object to the single hour of pleasure which the girl had found in it, when the proper care, which she alone could bestow, might have preserved it in its original condition for a lifetime.

How could Giselle, who considered herself so Bohemian in her tastes—visiting exhibitions of the latest paintings when they went up to Paris, apparently going into raptures about vividly-coloured nudes sighted through her lorgnettes, and even reading, with approval, a controversial novel about the suicide of an adulteress—how could she possibly have understood how delightful it was to watch an ignorant whore dress in *chic* clothes with a little less than full seriousness, when she dispatched their adopted son to bed the instant a ribald customer of Daniel's accepted a second glass of brandy?

With this girl, Daniel found, there were no complex feelings to circumvent. No subtle moods need be gauged. She hardly understood a word he was saying. Throwing a few piastres onto the bed he could simply leave, forgetting the occasional failure of the previous hour. He ignored her without impropriety.

Daniel sat up and looked into the dark. By his legs he could feel her warm body. Even his slight recoil from her black hair, spilling over the pillow, distastefully oily and thick, was curiously reassuring. Soon he would have escaped her atmosphere, without the elaborate ritual of bathing in silence. For in their marbled bathroom in Lyons the procedure had often prolonged the pain, just reconfirmed, of an inexpressible intimacy.

The girl put her hand on his knee. She pressed it very

tightly. Then raising herself up to his height, she kissed Daniel as violently as when he had entered. He patted her back, wondering what the time was. (An overpowering wave of sweat and sandalwood rose from her armpits.) He would not give her the extra piastres he had intended to leave. If he did she might suspect that he had decided never to return. Daniel had no wish to attend to her tears, nor to loiter in the hovel once their love-making had ended.

She would doubtless grow sentimental and morose. Certainly she had appeared to become torrid and difficult recently. She would dig her fingers, with their bitten nails, into his flesh and try to seem as though she were absorbing him with her large, expressionless eyes.

'DaLe! DaLe!' She would incantate what she could pronounce of his name. 'DaLe!' Over and over again she repeated it as if in passion.

'Shut up,' Daniel would whisper, putting a hand to her mouth. He knew very well that she spoke nothing but Arabic.

Finally he got up and fumbled in his frock-coat for his cigarette case. Why was it that life was so inconstant? He had never wished to disrupt his marriage with Giselle. Meeting this girl had simply enabled him to adapt to his highly-strung wife and welcome her growing remoteness. But then the whore whose indifference to him he had found initially reassuring, had begun to exhibit an embarrassing and superfluous devotion. And so the precarious balance of his existence seemed to alter.

With her pretence, impermissible and crude, to a savage love for Daniel the girl threatened to invade a world from which she had been carefully isolated. For Benchimol sought from her none of the loyalty and emotional finesse that was present, yet concealed, in his wife. She need not attempt, and fail, to display feelings which, like the subtlest tints on Giselle's Chinese silks, could only be discerned in certain rare lights.

Daniel sighed as he tapped the end of a cigarette on the gold case. He might have been willing to go on for ever with things as they were. His life, broken up into unconnected parts, each insufficient but indispensable, would have done. Every fragment had possessed a definite, if incomplete, kind of meaning. Of course, sometimes he had felt dissatisfied, it was true. A palpable centre for his conflicting impulses would have been more ideal. But then complete happiness was hardly a frequent human commodity. At least this way he could have escaped the sort of over-involvement which might have compromised his placidity and, most precious of all, his detachment.

Now even that confused order—he was sure he had not romanticized it—had crumbled. Those of his ships which remained were preparing to leave Alexandria for ever. While he himself would never again sail in the heat with a cargo of ripe cheeses, to visit the city, emptied of its frightened Europeans—his market, and an insignificant whore whose embraces were a trifle too insistent, and whom Daniel should remind himself he did not love.

How ironical it all was! No sooner had one achieved what one hoped would be a stable situation, seeing clearly the pattern of one's life, perceiving the best that circumstances would permit, than events invalidated one's wisdom. And looking back at the girl who was now sitting up watching him sadly—or so he imagined—in the dark, Daniel realized how infrequently one possessed the resolution to heed one's own insights. Perhaps he would give her the extra piastres after all.

'Sometimes things seem to get better, but then they grow worse.' He remembered, almost with fondness, the Doctor, his blemished face flushed with champagne, talking loudly on the afternoon of Albert Grimaud's wedding. 'Usually they grow worse.' Everyone there had laughed. Even the old father gave a weak smile. After all, it was a festive occasion.

Visible from the reception room in Catherine's house, over the lawn and through the still garden, were Egyptians leading camels and mules on the beach. They slowly loaded sand into raffia baskets fixed to the saddles. While others, painfully working among the ruined parts of the Arab quarter with bodies racked by choleric coughs, filled sacks with the newly-acquired material. Then, banking them up among charred rubble and in the remnants of drains, they gazed at the British gunboat as they prepared for a further attack.

'Life's an uncertain business. You never know when you're going to be on top . . .' The speeches echoed, uninterrupted, through the room with its high ceiling.

The guests, easily grouped into a corner by the bride's mother, were all quiet, fatigued by the heat and champagne. They turned from each successive speaker to stare at the unoccupied floor.

The table, a horse-shoe promontory of embroidered linen, reached into the elegant emptiness. Porcelain bonbonieres, decorated with eighteenth-century shepherds and shepherdesses painted against harmonious landscapes, were unopened. Two-thirds of the silver salvers and dishes were virtually untouched. The only changes since the morning seemed to be that the running gelatine of the *Boeuf à la mode* set the carrot roses adrift, and that the ice buckets, scented with orange blossoms, were now awash with tepid water.

Daniel caught himself looking out of the window as he delivered his own few words. Cargo was being loaded in the dockyard. He even made out the battered hulk of what had been, until recently, one of his own ships.

'On this happy occasion I should like to wish Catherine and Albert all the prosperity they deserve . . .'

Agitated Europeans, not a few of whom had doubtless sent an affirmative reply to the wedding invitation, were scuttling away from the custom's shed. Making for various gangplanks, they set down bulging valises and nervously searched inside pockets for tickets, passports, and other identification.

How soon would it be, Daniel wondered, before the sombre gentlemen whom he was now facing, with their bushy moustaches and diamond cravat pins, would try to fit a lifetime of successful business into a single suitcase and dab the sweat from their necks on the quay? . . .

Albert was standing just beside Benchimol, solemnly fingering the gold watch chain which fed his waistcoat pocket. His dark hair, slightly pomaded with lavender, was boldly brushed back from his forehead.

'I've known Albert for many years, in fact since he was quite a small boy. Even then it was obvious that he was the sort of person who would only be satisfied with the best.'

The bride's mother took the remark to conceal a compliment to herself through the medium of her daughter. Other ladies, including great aunts wearing black dresses and other festive garments, carried on her obvious satisfaction by smiling at one another and even at Catherine, delicately veiled in stifling white.

M. Grimaud, immaculately dressed in clothes twenty years out of fashion, attended to the hostess now no more than he had during the reception. From his chair, surrounded by bosoms, he preferred to eye his own son. He would gently nod his silvered head, almost as if to reassure Albert. The medallion he had received for services to the French people swayed from his frail, though curiously distinguished, neck.

Daniel remembered M. Grimaud sitting in silence several weeks previous to the wedding. The old man had observed his son's negotiations with Benchimol in the study with the same watchful, though controlled expression. He hardly interrupted when Albert tried to persuade Benchimol to rescind part of the shipping agreement by bullying in an embarrassingly amateurish fashion. Nor did Grimaud's expression grow appreciably less benign as it became clear that the youth assumed Daniel was morally bound to comply with his wishes because his marriage was, in some way, 'inevitable'.

What exceptional patience the old man must have had to tolerate such arrogance and conceit! For all his obvious nervousness—continually shifting his position and crossing and recrossing his legs—he seemed to have achieved a kind of internal balance which his son's antics could do little to upset. This was the sort of repose, Daniel imagined, achieved by turning inwards over the course of many years, away from the partial and un-related satisfactions of an increasingly meaningless life.

How could Albert, in all but age a mere boy, under-stand or respect such serenity? He had never known the difficulties of salvaging, even imperfectly, a quiet sanctum for one's personality from the shrill voices of a harsh and hostile world. He believed in, clung to, the goal of complete happiness. He thought that to desire it suf-ficiently intensely would necessarily guarantee attainment to such an improbable ideal.

His love for Catherine and his engagement apparently so dominated Albert's emotions that it never occurred to him that they might be less real to others than to himself. Yet in time, Daniel reflected, when the youth's affections had faltered, the imperative mood of these feelings would imperceptibly wane. Attachments and needs which had once surely directed the universe, would appear rather more relative. They might seem too grandiose.

Then what a plummeting to earth! How hard the fall would be. And with what despair the youth would finally come to himself . . . but until that day Albert would remain as self-deceived as he had been during their interview.

Could he really believe that his remarks about Catherine were so absorbing? Lovers' lectures on their beloved were, after all, a genre to which Daniel was hardly susceptible. The high seriousness with which Albert spoke of his *fiancée*'s qualities, and the humourlessness which informed his apparently indestructible love for her, would be even more intolerable if it were not for that sense of irony which allowed Daniel to smile prophetically at the inescapable future of all these passions.

'Dust and ashes. Dust and ashes. That's what you turn everything to with your scepticism,' LeGrand had once said in the old days. 'By the time you're middle-aged you'll have killed all your joy in the world with your spite.'

But then that was the sort of remark which an embittered old Doctor could be expected to make. And Benchimol was certain that his criticisms of Albert's obsessional love merely derived from the fact that such squandered emotion made him seem slightly ridiculous. Besides, one soon grew insensitive to the existence of others; good manners entirely dissolved. Even the most provincial French businessman could affect more charm than Albert showed.

Who, for example, would have dreamt of breaking a gentleman's agreement? Albert did so on the scant grounds that a handshake could never be legally binding. The clause relevant to Benchimol's long-term purchase of the remaining ships had not yet been entered into the contract. And, like an Arab, Albert refused to admit that the delay had been caused by his own father's indifference.

Yet Daniel had already been using the two vessels for some time. They were now an integral part of his business. He had even put the legal document in his inside pocket when he left the hotel to visit Grimaud over in Ramleh. (It was the original of those copies which he fruitlessly sent from France for the old man's signature, together with affectionate letters which Giselle, always the natural hostess, was so good at writing.)

With the official consolidation of his fleet, Daniel had hoped to withdraw his commerce altogether from the diseased and troublesome city.

'But you *must* return them,' Albert insisted when Benchimol stated that the ships in question could not be recalled for some time. Apparently one was in dry dock in Marseilles and the other, at present floating somewhere off the coast of Calabria, was destined for the Adriatic. 'You must learn to honour your obligations.' Grimaud only reacted to his son's absurd moralizing with a helpless wince, despite an outraged glance from Benchimol.

'But I really don't see what I can do. After all, you've hardly given me much time to prepare for your extraordinary change of mind.'

'Well, you must do something. It will take long enough, as it is, to realize even a part of the full cash value of those ships. Besides, our buyer can't afford to wait for ever. Providing transport for the whole Jewish community is a terrible problem.' Albert could not look more adult and serious. 'And it's a job that needs to be done *now*.'

As the wrangling continued, Benchimol repeatedly turned to Grimaud for support or at least some sign of sympathy. And as Albert grew more and more intransigent, Daniel would turn to the father and inquire testily if he shared his son's position. The old man did not answer but shrugged his shoulders, raising his eyebrows as if to say, 'What can I do?'

Surrendering to his son—it seemed to Benchimol both then and now—had been Solomon Grimaud's folly.

'In that case, all I can suggest,' Benchimol said coldly after some time, exhausted by Albert's abrasiveness, 'is that I return one of the ships—but I can only do that when it's finished in the Adriatic. It's a terrible nuisance but since you're so insistent I suppose I'll have to. As for the other one, I can't do a thing at the moment. It's in dry dock and there it must stay, I'm afraid. But I could replace it, if you're willing, with another ship—the *Aboukir*—which is here in Alexandria . . .'

'Well that sounds like the solution,' Albert said, obviously delighted.

'Let me add,' Benchimol continued, holding up an index finger with an air of stern candour, 'that you may feel the *Aboukir* requires certain repairs, and if you're pressed for time . . .'

'But does it float?' Albert asked, his relief blossoming into heavy humour.

'Oh yes, b . . .'

Albert rose impulsively. Within a minute his brusque manner cut short the discussion of details. And having extended his right hand, which Benchimol shook rather diffidently, he had made it quite clear that the tense interview was at an end.

Now that the *Aboukir* had been finally returned, Daniel could look through the window, during the wedding reception, and hardly regret losing the squalid craft, with its ugly smoke stack and squat, ill-painted hull. At least he had not allowed Albert to deprive him of the intrinsically superior ship—now languishing, it was true—in Marseilles. He had surely emerged from the whole affair pretty well.

Not that there was anything seriously wrong with the *Aboukir*. Daniel himself had sailed on it this time to Egypt. Although there had certainly been recurrent engine troubles, nerve-racking noises and constant stops, he eventually arrived. Daniel was no engineer, and could not say for certain, but imagined that all defects could soon be repaired—that is if they could procure the spare parts. Besides, presumably the Grimauds knew the quirks of what had once been one of their own craft. If the *Aboukir* was too unseaworthy it was their responsibility, not his, to withdraw it from service . . .

'Thank God I shan't be coming back,' Daniel thought to himself. He was now dressed, staring into the patch of stifling darkness in which he could hear the Arab girl slipping into her frock. He drew on a cigarette and sighed deeply as he exhaled. He was releasing all the anxiety which had grown up during these past few weeks: he had been struggling to settle, once and for all, his affairs in Alexandria.

Soon he would be standing on board ship, free, alone, his face in the evening breeze. He would look at the stars reflected in the Mediterranean.

As she moved towards him, Daniel could see the girl's eyes. He handed her a bunch of wrinkled bank notes. (He had intended to give her fewer.) He bestowed a perfunctory kiss on her forehead in order to forestall a passionate embrace. He turned to the door softly. Maybe he was a little sad. He scarcely noticed something, perhaps an insect, brush the side of his face.

The money fell from his shoulder. Saliva was rolling down his sleeve. The girl had begun shrieking in Arabic.

She threw something hard at his head. Two other whores were banging on the door. They forced their way into the room. Then a man in an alley shouted:

'You think you clever! All French go—but first you pay!'

Benchimol cried out for help. He was hit on the side of the head.

They were about to set sail sometime later. Benchimol arrived, without his luggage or hat. Both watch and money were missing. His shirt sleeves hung loosely out of his jacket. The cuff-links had been torn off. And his collar flapped ineffectively: the back stud must have been too difficult to rip out.

He rubbed a hand over his temple. It was sore. The hair was splintered with glass. And the sickening smell of sandalwood had spread from his head to his neck.

As Daniel struggled up the narrow gangplank he caught a glimpse of the moon. Its palid light seemed like a fire, burning the bleeding tissues which sealed off his left eye.

PART IV
Over a Year Later

New Beginnings

Chapter 12

Grimaud could hardly see the city now. A mere few minutes previously he had made out individual buildings. The edges of minarets and Ras-el-Tin had stood severe against the brilliant sky. And the jagged green of palm fronds seemed clear, across the water, in the gardens of deserted houses.

For a moment Grimaud imagined that he could see beyond the curve of Stanley Bay. Surely that little wall, vivid with geraniums, backed his own villa left with a servant to sell . . . But the colours now merged; the swell increased gently; and the whole length of Alexandria seemed to fade into a line.

The ship turned outwards towards the sea. A regular thud drowned the high-pitched shrieks of children. They chased hoops between groups of silent adults who still watched the spaces which had just contained their homes, as if stunned. But despite the shouting, the waves and the continual calling of gulls, Grimaud pictured a noiseless city. He saw Alexandria without people or motion, as it had been from a distance, only a moment before.

Perhaps it was the wide, untroubled sky which helped him to forget the crowds around the statue in Mohammed Ali Square. Arabs, all in white, had punctuated speeches with their roars; while wasted bodies, with large staring eyes, were left to gasp for water in isolated huts, still quarantined.

Maybe the clean, salt sea had rid his memory of the agonizing choice of whether to leave or to remain. Alone now that Albert and Catherine were in Paris, he had asked himself again and again if he should allow his life to be disrupted by the gathering political storm; or might it be better to make a fresh start in one of the new Jewish agricultural settlements in Palestine?

The Doctor had occasionally sat with him.

'The epidemic's passing, so that's less of a reason,' LeGrand would say. 'Of course in a sewer like that,' he pointed away vaguely, 'there'll always be a few cases left. It's your choice, but I'm staying. It's inertia I suppose. Besides, would it really be better anywhere else?'

Even the rush at the last minute, his impulse to escape while staring from the balcony at the imperturbable water a mere twenty-four hours ago, had faded from his mind. The breeze, catching up the grey hairs from his temples, seemed to carry off his recollection of booking a passage. The ships had been so full that he had even had to pay a bribe for a berth on the *Aboukir*.

So in the space of a moment, as if time were suspended, he saw the city of his life. The trees and walls, which he had always lived with, appeared in each of their stages all at once. Every impulse and sensation which had made up his substance stood real, connected, and strange. As in dreams he both was, and could know from a distance, the past and the present. Sheer memory had lifted like a veil.

In that clearness, unimpaired by the usual limitations of prejudice or circumstance, his emotions became simple and true. He could now tell with an implacable certainty of things which he had previously glimpsed but shunned.

He even found, in this same instant, the courage to contemplate his anger with his son. (At the time he had allowed his ill-humour to pass into resigned tolerance without complicated explanations—least of all to himself.) He could have written to Albert, now married for over

a year, that his spite at the engagement was the sole
channel allowed to his feelings by his pride. It diverted
his horror at the prospect of being abandoned; for how
could he have borne to feel so dispensable and worthless? He knew too, though not for the first time, that
panic had caused his rages with Ivette. His fear of the
emotional paralysis he experienced in her presence had
expressed itself in outbursts of fury.

Other situations—with his father, his mother—grew
lucid; he saw them whole. He had often half-remembered
them, but they seemed too disquieting. He realized that
he had dismissed them out of anxiety. Yet the panic,
the terror, to which he was subject (or more simply the
nervousness: cold shivers and headaches) no longer
deadened his awareness and dulled his brain. He seemed
to have come upon some reserve of strength in himself,
though not the heroic power he had once extolled.

Grimaud must have thought of these things for more
than a minute. He had been looking at the horizon for
so long that the sky merged into the sea. Their intangible
mixture, neither mere air nor water, was continuous
with his mood. He did not sleep, but in his reverie he
was not conscious of being awake.

He felt, for some reason, calmed by considering the
experiences which had once given him pain. A pacific
sensation, like warm waves, flowed uninterrupted between
him and the spaces beyond. There was nothing he need
banish; nothing was too terrible. All ushered in an
imperishable wholeness. He was fused with the entire
world.

Later he began to feel faint. The wind had risen. The
light was waning. It was as if some life-force were drain-
ing out of him, drop by drop.

Of course he had known it before. Climbing the stairs
to his bedroom, he felt his foot refuse the next step.
Lifting a cup to his lips, he noticed the lop-sided coffee
quiver at the rim, a hand already dead in his lap. There
was the occasional unsteadiness as he moved from the
heat to the shade. And even simply sitting, perhaps in

this deck-chair, he wondered whether his thoughts, now drifting, would return to such heavy limbs.

Sometimes, as now, the peaceful dozing grew more urgent. He was exhilarated by a strange tremor of life. Liberated from the downward pull of his body his spirits soared. He was free. Then with excitement rising, trembling as if violently ill, he seemed to leave all confinement for ever. He was entering the ultimate reaches . . .

There was darkness. The ship's motor was deafening. The deck rail had started to vibrate. The whole hull was grating and grinding. There was complete silence when the engines were turned off.

After floating free for a time in the moonlight, the *Aboukir* sounded its bell. The ringing continued more urgently when the main explosion occurred.

Panic-stricken families, gathering on the foredeck, ignored the old man, still in his deck-chair, his head slumped over his chest.

Chapter 13

Albert had always dreaded such occasions. They were so formal and grave. Yet he would never have entertained the idea of not attending. His presence was indispensable now.

As he put on his black coat he pulled the shirt cuffs clear of his sleeves. He adjusted his collar. One should dress impeccably for functions like these.

He reached into his pocket to make sure he had the text of his speech. It was written out fully and he knew it virtually by heart. He could imagine nothing worse than growing tongue-tied when his turn came to address the other gentlemen. Albert could almost see the Baron Edmond de Rothschild's stern expression, as he glanced into his dressing-room mirror.

M. Gabai had assured Albert, some days earlier, that

only the most distinguished French Jews would attend the annual Zionist dinner. He was unfolding the seating plan, unasked, in the library of Albert's house in the *Rue St. Sulpice*. Then, just as the young man was amusing himself with the thought of this uneducated businessman, hardly settled in Paris, earnestly posing as eminent and French, Gabai pointed to the name *M. Grimaud*, placed among the speakers at the head table.

'For services to the advancement of Zionism.' Gabai tapped the relevant spot solemnly. Albert was now standing up straight, his hands locked behind him.

'But it's a great honour,' Catherine remarked later that afternoon. She leaned forward in her chair and steadied their small son. He nearly fell down each time he stumbled into the rays of autumn light which slanted through the drawing-room window.

Albert listened remotely as his wife pointed out the social advantages that would doubtless ensue; the respect to which they would both be entitled. He merely smiled in his usual vague way when she looked up, paused, and then said, 'Well, you don't seem to be very happy.'

Naturally Albert realized that he should be overjoyed at receiving the general acclamation, which he had always courted, with such ease. Yet, lounging on the chaise longue, he could only feel the most distant sensation of victory. As the evening wore on, his mood grew so detached from any reminiscence of pleasure that he stared from the sofa in his study with an appearance almost of anguish.

As Albert composed his address his mind grew continually blank. He was struggling to order momentous thoughts on this second flight from Egypt. But rereading each new paragraph, he despaired of its hectoring tone. And when pruning the more inelegant expressions in a passage concerning the Red Sea, he suffered from acute cramp in his fingers. His entire body had been flooded with darkness and pain . . .

At least the address was now written. Albert consoled himself with the thought as he drew a folded sheet of paper from his inside pocket. Yet this was not the speech, which he now noticed lying over a pair of hair-brushes on the dressing-table. It was Mme Benchimol's letter, absentmindedly left in the jacket a day or so previously.

Albert re-read the black-edged note quickly. Giselle regretted not having expressed her sympathy sooner at M. Grimaud's death in the *Aboukir* disaster. Her husband had only just been able to trace Albert's Paris address. They had both been very fond of the old man and were appalled to think that his well-deserved retirement, away from the stresses of recent years, should have been curtailed in such an arbitrary way.

Albert did not care to read on. He allowed the folded letter to fall from his fingers, and watched it float into the wastepaper basket with an air of distaste.

Was it really credible, after all, that Benchimol should have taken well over a year to contact him? Surely it was no coincidence that the insurance company required a good twelve months to work out the indemnities on the wreck. For, as the distraught Gabai pointed out to Albert some time ago, it was obvious that M. Grimaud had been entitled to the return of a vessel; but what was less clear was whether Benchimol had renounced legal ownership of the *Aboukir* by attempting, without contract, to offer it in lieu of the original ship. Now that Gabai's claim was decisively vindicated by the insurance investigators—and how delighted he had been!; his son had said there was nothing his father would not do for Albert—Benchimol, or rather his wife, probably considered that little would be lost by a conventional, if belated, show of sympathy.

It went without saying that Benchimol had been almost criminal in attempting to reclaim the ship despite his definite, albeit unwritten, surrender of the vessel. Yet what shocked Albert even more was that Benchimol had been prepared to exchange the *Aboukir*, well aware of its defects, and thus profit by the danger to its passengers. What could be the state of mind of a man who coldly calculated his business returns in terms of deaths, like that of Albert's father? What twisted, self-deceptions would he fall prey to in his attempts to undo his feelings of guilt?

There was a sense, Albert considered, as he put the sheets of paper in his pocket, in which his address would commemorate his father. Though the old man had not been perfect—after all, nobody was—Albert would always remember him as he had once been: strong willed, uncompromising, and with a sterling character . . .

Again he felt the pains which had recurred recently. The darkness welled up in his head. Probably, he told himself as the door bell rang to announce that M. Gabai was waiting outside for him in his carriage, it was just the nervousness which everyone felt before an important banquet.

Chapter 14

LeGrand paused for a moment before leaving the grave-side. The flowers, roses and lilies, seemed fragile against the dry mound. Wreaths, their glistening leaves neatly interlaced, were already limp in the unremitting heat. Soon they would be driven forward by the burning wind, together with the other branches and twigs which scratched the surface of Chatby.

The Doctor did not linger to console the relatives and friends. He had hardly known the deceased or her husband. They were part of that new generation of Europeans which had settled in Alexandria now that the worst of the epidemics and riots was past. LeGrand had been called after the lady had already suffered the worst of her heart attacks. It was the first time in over ten years that he had re-entered the villa which once belonged to Solomon Grimaud.

Occasionally, during that time, he recognized some item of furniture in a patient's home. He might find himself sitting by an invalid in a chair whose arms culminated in eagles' heads; their golden forms would be obscured in the suffocating gloom. And once he noticed, from the window of a bedroom where a man had recently died, a statuette standing in the overgrown garden. Geraniums were sprouting inside Napoleon's cracked head.

Like these relics, LeGrand considered, M. Grimaud's remains were scattered far and wide. He had never been buried; he now shared the sea bed. Who in the future would know that he had ever lived? He had no tombstone or memorial. Perhaps he was already a handful of pebbles on the beach.

At least, the Doctor reflected as the family moved away from the grave, the line would be borne on by Albert. The old man would surely have been proud of the increased honour attached to his name. Albert Grimaud was now mentioned in the same breath as Edmond de Rothschild by people who discussed leading Zionists. And perhaps, like all fathers, M. Grimaud had left more than a trace of his personality in his son. How fine it must be to have children; to know that one would always survive through them. It was almost a process of nature, like the continual renewal of the earth.

The Doctor turned back before the others. He passed the Catholic priest who was wearily disrobing, folding the funerary vestments in the inadequate shade of a palm. Some of its fronds hung in nearly colourless splinters. Others lay inert where they had fallen. There they would stay, unabsorbed by the sterile sand.